Eric & Izzy

A Witches & Immortals Prequel
Book 3

Stephanie Vorwald

Copyright © 2023 Stephanie Vorwald

ISBN: 979-8-9893169-1-5

Editing by Whitney Morsillo of Whitney's Book Works

Cover Design by Etheric Tales & Edits

Butterfly Chapter Headers by Sweet 15 Designs- Taylor Dawn

This prequel is dedicated to my cover designers: Etheric Designs. Out of pure luck, I won this cover as a milestone giveaway. As soon as I saw the cover, I knew exactly the story I needed to write. A villain backstory is always a must and thankfully the story flowed perfectly into the Witches & Immortals book series exactly how I hoped it would.

When I first started writing this book in high school, I knew I wanted it to be four books total, and because of the love and support from fans, family, and friends, I was able to continue this series.

I hope you enjoy my cup of tea as much as I do.

Witches & Immortals Series

Book 1: Witches & Immortals
Book 2: Secrets & Thyme (Sequel)
Book 3: Eric & Izzy (Prequel)
Book 4: Bonds & Bones (Finale)

Isadora Cambridge

I knew I'd be dead by sundown. Unless by some lucky chance the old gods were having a day of games and wanted to play with my luck, using my life as their prize.

In that case… my death would be final by tomorrow's sunrise.

I swallowed hard at the thought as I woke with the warm sun coming through the window, touching my face, and the slight breeze blowing through my hair. The bed stuffed with hay and animal hides wasn't as comfortable as the field I had fallen asleep in last night. I prayed that it was my mother that carried me back home to my room and not Eric. I hadn't planned on coming back home, and if it had been Eric, then I would kill him for not letting me get as far away as possible.

To be fair… he had no idea what I was even running from. If he knew, he would've been running with me. Far, far away.

Ragnar, my pathetic, cowardly father, was going to be furious when he found out what I did.

My sister and I had been the first born Anchor twins, and my father resented us from the day we were born. We had been born with unimaginable power that we were still trying to perfect. Our father scoffed every time he watched us conjure a small flame or water wisps in our palms. "Childish magic" was what he called it, and it was nothing more than a waste of time to him. We were to be powerful and conquer the lands for him. Not just some of the lands, but *all* lands.

A shiver ran through my spine as I thought of him.

He was chaotic, and I truly wanted nothing to do with such a powerless human.

My sister and I were the only ones of our kind. We had a special bond that kept us balanced. The earth seemed to like the balance as well. I syphoned while she healed. It was a sick little game our ancestors played with us. But if our ancestors were anything like our father, then I got it, he would forever wish ill on us, and I was sure his family before him felt the same.

When we were born, our father lost his own magic, they called it chaos magic, though I had never seen the power he could actually perform. I was still unsure if that was a good thing to have missed. All I knew was that he wouldn't stop torturing us until he had his chaos magic back, and for some reason, he believed that Mags and I could get it back for him.

He always had another power of mind manipulation, which was ruined on our day of birth. Unfortunately, he slowly began to regain that buzzing in our ears but hadn't seemed to fully tap into it yet. For all of our sakes, I hoped it stayed that way.

He always believed that one of us was hiding his power in our mind, but neither me nor my sister even knew how to get into our own minds the way he was rumored to. We all knew that he had clearly gone mad, and he'd stop at nothing to get all of his chaos back, no matter the cost.

The witching universe punished him for reasons that our mother refused to discuss with us. She believed we were still too young to understand. She continued to keep her distance from him and only tended to Mags and me to keep herself busy.

Luckily for me, our father wouldn't be back home until sundown. So, if today was my last day, then I was going to make the best of it.

"Mags, come on, please come with me… We are still kids, we deserve to have some fun!" I said, tugging under her arm and trying to use my non-existent mind melding on her. "Please," I begged, as I stepped away from her and looked out the window, trying to hide my pleading smirk. "Before I die tonight," I whispered under my breath while praying that she would just agree and come with me to the Greystone land.

I wanted to fight Eric in a rematch from last week. He cheated, and I wanted a fair fight and bragging rights. His older brother, Jimmy, tackled me and rolled me down the rocky bluffs just as I was about to win, and that wasn't fair. Eric didn't deserve the title of sword fighting king, I did. Only because I am a girl do they tend to push me aside as if my strengths didn't matter at all. It was only fair that if I was going to die tonight, I would get one last good beating in on someone and let my tomb in the cave say 'Izzy Champion of all kingdoms.' We all knew that I had no chance against my father, magicless or not he would strangle me just for looking at him wrong. So, Eric was my only shot that was semi equivalent to my doom.

"We can't today," she answered, annoyed by my request. "We're only twelve, but we have responsibilities. The garden needs to be tended before we can plant for spring. Mother won't approve."

"Ugh, if you're not a mini version of Mother herself then I don't know who is." I pushed her back in a playful manner and began my damsel in distress act while falling back onto her bed, which was much softer than mine with the fur and feathers from Sir Greystone's son, Jimmy, as a gift for helping mend the growing fields and splitting the land with us. Two rulers on one land was not common, but for Crystal Rock it worked. Peace was more important than a title in these days of sickness and death.

"It's just that… oh, never mind."

"It's just that what?" she perked up.

It was then that I knew that I had her attention locked in, and I had her little heart wrapped around my finger.

"Oh, nothing. Just a secret."

"Come on, Izzy, tell me! Please!"

I smirked, knowing that she would give me whatever I wanted for a secret. "I mustn't."

"You must!" she pleaded.

"Fine, agree to come with me, and I'll tell you."

"Fine! I'll come with you."

I smiled and sat up. "So, rumor has it that Sir Greystone's son has a thing for a blonde headed twin," I lied.

She gasped. "Which son?"

"Jimmy, of course," I announced, knowing that she had been swooning over him for months now, and this was sure to get her to follow me.

She blushed as I'm sure her imagination wandered. A stupid boy was going to ruin the power Mags had, and she didn't even realize it. Her heart was too big for her little body. She needed to accept that her and I were destined for great things together and not let a stupid boy get between us.

"Okay, fine. But we have to be back before Father gets home."

I nodded, agreeing to the terms even though I was debating on running away tonight, and I hoped that she would want to join me, but now I knew that I was alone, yet again.

I walked back to my room and packed a small sack of dried fruit and grain, just in case I needed a quick getaway. I quickly placed the broken Jasper stone into the sack and prayed that Eric might know how to mend it with his magic so that I could replace it before Father noticed. It would be my last hope of surviving tonight.

I ran to the nearby river and filled the jug with water before sealing it and packing it away in the sack. I yelled for Mags to hurry up so we would have the full day of light before the raging moon and Father would be back from trying to scavenge more magical objects. A part of me prayed that he wouldn't return home. A quick dagger to his poisoned heart would do just fine. My shameful thoughts were surely to be tested by the gods, dooming me out of Valhalla for good, but if I kept my thoughts secret, never speaking aloud of my hatred toward him, then maybe… just maybe the gods would forgive me. I just wished my father would conquer another land far, far away and stay to watch it thrive. But most likely, with him around, it would burn, depending on his mood that day.

I slung the sack over my shoulder and secured my dull sword to the sheath that would surely make me king of all of Crystal Rock and not just the stupid field of Greystone land. Maybe I could even claim the sacred cave too—carve my name into the wall in the back where no one would see it but me, and it would be my little piece of land. Mags ran up next to me, bringing my daydreaming back to reality, carrying a satchel of herbs.

"What's that for?" I asked, annoyed at the extra baggage that I would surely have to carry.

"Mother said to bring it to Lady Greystone for her garden."

I huffed. "You told her that we were going back there?"

Mags stared back at me in frustration. "Was I not supposed to?"

"Ugh," I huffed. "Can't you just keep a secret to yourself for once?"

I grabbed her arm and dragged her along, knowing that I hurt her feelings. But she didn't understand that if our father came home sooner and found out that I broke his Jasper fossil in half, he would surely drown me in the river after Mother went to sleep. It was the only piece of magic that he'd found in years to try to bring his own magic back. He was waiting for the planets to align before trying to use it. I didn't want my mother to be involved by knowing where we were. I needed to try one more remedy before confessing. Then, my mother would surely blame herself for my own actions. I needed to catch him off guard and not the other way around to keep the advantage of assessing his temper before entering the home. Now he could just come to beat me on another's land, which could start another war between the families.

Stupid sister.

Mags walked silently next to me, knowing that she had upset me.

Good, I thought. Sometimes I wished that I was an only child. Having to share a life and my magic with her was not always easy. Plus, who knew, maybe if I was just a single born witch, our father would still have his magic and wouldn't hate me so much for thinking I syphoned his. I shook my head, letting the thoughts disappear.

I love my sister.

"I'm sorry, Mags," I said, wrapping my arm around her shoulder as we walked.

Chapter 2
Eric Greystone

"Damn it, Jimmy. I already told you I didn't want to go by them today. Izzy doesn't stop until I finally let her win."

"Come on, brother. Please. It's the only way I get to see Mags."

I huffed at his stupidity. If he liked the girl enough, then he should just ask her to be his. Our parents would be happy to officially seal the land by joining our families. It was what they wanted to do for years. Jimmy was only two years older than Mags and me, and surely, she was wiser than her winter years. The two of them could get married in the cave and carve their names on the wall as a final pact of alliance, then maybe the surrounding Norse assholes could stop trying to take what was ours. There would be no chance of seizing our land if we had the alliance we needed. He needed to marry her and make little strong warriors so that I wouldn't have to do any such thing.

I wanted to roam the lands and be free.

Explore.

I was tired of my duty to protect and kill only because I was good at it. Jimmy was the eldest, he should be next in line. But no, my swordsmanship sealed my fate. I always knew I should've been the older brother. My maturity had always been beyond his.

"Fine, if I meet her in the field, will you quiet your mouth already? Mother isn't going to like us taking the swords from Father's room again."

He nodded, and we left for the field.

I gritted my teeth, knowing that I was going to let her win today so she would finally stop trying to prove herself to everyone. She was so worried about being someone important for her father's approval that she would surely never get it because no one could please Ragnar Cambridge nor could I believe that her goddess of a mother ever slept with the man to bear children to begin with. Rumor had it that he used his mind control to get her into his chambers and take over her land from under her father's rule, quite conveniently before her mother and father grew ill from a new disease that only killed them.

Ragnar already pulled me aside last week and told me he would slice my ears off the next time I laid my hands on his eldest. Of course, I took the blame to cover for my brother's ass for rolling down the bluffs with her. But in fairness, it was only in defense from her trying to kick the shit out of me. I would just have to be careful not to leave any visible marks this time, otherwise we were both dead. Ragnar was not one to mess with.

Jimmy and I spent last winter with their family to learn their ways of how to act with ladies in the house while my mother and father had to take the river by longship to lands too far to travel for an immortality spell my mother had been trying to perfect. Before we went to stay with them, other families on our lands warned me of him and his mind games. There was a wickedness to him that no one wanted to cross. It was then that I perfected keeping him the hell out of my head.

"Come on, let's go." I grabbed Jimmy, and we headed for the open field to seal our fate with the twins.

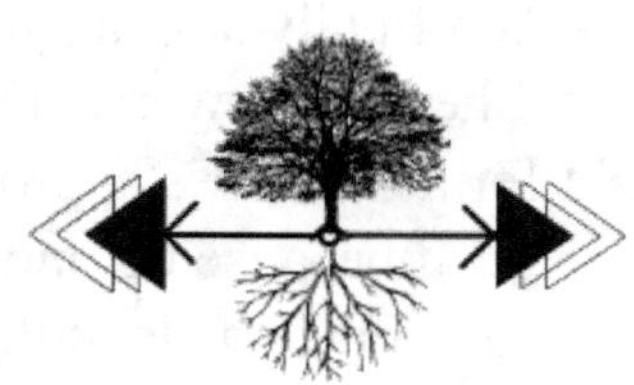

There she was, standing next to the lonely tree that was still too small to give any good shade, waiting for me to battle. This girl was never going to stop until she won.

I huffed heavily as I made my way to her, annoyed with each step.

She wanted to beat me? Me?

Eric, the great. The youngest warrior to have won every battle next to Father. A child, but a man with my sword.

Our mother had always been so worried about our safety that she continued to work on that stupid immortality protection spell. Something that was trial and error at this point, but eventually, she was hoping to make my brother and I fully immortal.

The loss of another child was something that she just couldn't bear, and I didn't blame her because I didn't think I could handle that form of loss, either. To give the breath of life to a child and raise them only to lose them before they pass on the family name would be tragic. An heir was the most important duty a man could fulfill. Luckily for our father, he received two boys, but unfortunately for Ragnar, he received two daughters and no one to carry on his awful legacy.

Pity.

I laughed to myself.

Our mother still has not forgiven herself for our sister passing away last year. Who was to know that she would take her first steps in the middle of the night and head to the river. The fierce water swept her away before anyone had even noticed. It wasn't until daylight the next morning that she was found on the side bank near the horses. That day our mother swore that she would not lose another child. My battles had paused since that day, and she kept her nose buried deep in her grandmother's grimoire, and late night gatherings with the elders were becoming too frequent. But what she was trying to do would come with a price. A price that I wasn't too eager to pay, but I already knew that I would have no choice in the matter. I was an obeying son and a man of my word.

Immortality sounded like a great thing until all of my loved ones passed on to Valhalla and would leave me behind for an eternity to mourn them. The gods would never agree to letting a child live an immortal life. Our mother needed to grieve as we had and move on. Or maybe do as Jimmy and I did and let our minds get distracted enough while in battles with Father instead of trying to use spells and hexes. My life shouldn't be longer than it was meant to be.

What if my future immortality made me lose my place in Valhalla with my baby sister and I never saw her again?

"Daydreaming about me again?" Izzy walked up and sneered. "I'm going to beat you today, fair and square." She tied her braids back. "I need that spell to fix something I broke."

I laughed. "Izzy, I was kidding. I don't have a spell. But I can give you this sword if you win." She glanced at the glimmer and realized I had brought a sharp sword instead of the childish dull ones we had been playing with.

"How—" she stammered. "How did you get that?"

"It's my very own. From my first battle. My father forged it from dragon's blood after we won. It's filled with enormous magic of its own." I tilted it back and forth to show the shimmering blood embedded. I knew that she would only stop if there was a prize at stake besides bragging rights. "And it can be all yours if you win. Under one condition." She watched me intently, but her eyes flickered back to the prize. "No more sword fighting after today. Ragnar—"

She smirked, cutting me off. "Done." She spat in her hand and waited to seal the deal.

I mimicked her as we shook.

"Yes, I know. My father is a bastard man and will slice off your ears if you leave another mark." She laughed as she imitated Ragnar's tone.

"Izzy, it's not a laughing matter. Your father is—"

"Crazy? Yes, I know. That's why I need to win that magic sword." She shifted uncomfortably, and fear flooded her eyes.

"What's happened?"

She turned, and I watched as she quickly wiped a tear. "Nothing, let's just get this over with."

She pulled out her dull sword and took a stance. I turned and looked over my shoulder at Jimmy and Mags sitting next to the tree, watching intently. They seemed to be six feet apart but wanting to both be closer in proximity. I laughed to myself as I watched their awkwardness.

Stupid kids.

Izzy didn't wait as she jumped in the air and swung her sword near my throat. I pushed her back midair and pulled my dull edged sword from behind my back, tossing the prized dragon's sword to the side of the field. It pierced the ground, standing upright and shimmering in the sun. I took my wooden sword and slammed harder against hers, giving myself a fair stance. She smirked as she advanced again.

Something was bothering her. I watched as her anger took charge and knew she wanted more than a mere play fight. She wanted blood, and for whatever reason, she was staying silent about it. I wish I knew what was in her head. She was lovely behind the brutal ignorance of wanting to always win. I grabbed her arm, and my body jolted into another dimension. The field began to spin as my body traveled through time and I landed in another place entirely.

I tried to focus my eyes as I watched Izzy picking up the Jasper stone, and it glowed with her touch. Her hands shook as her eyes widened. She frantically dropped the stone, and it broke in two pieces, revealing a fossil. I walked closer as I tried to study the stone. Izzy panicked and held the two pieces back together, trying to will it to become whole again. "No, no, no. He's going to kill me. Father is going to strangle me when he sees this. I need to leave. I need to take the stone and run before he's home." She grabbed the two pieces and darted toward her bed-chamber before hiding it under her pillow. "Eric knows some spells… maybe he can help," she whispered frantically to herself and prepared a sack of daily needs as if she planned on actually running away. I watched as her emotions went haywire.

My eyes widened as the field came back into view, and Izzy's sword was swinging a mere inch from my face before she hit me hard. It was too late—she had caught me off guard, knocking me on my back. I caught myself with my elbows before my head cracked on the ground. I tried to refocus on the field and bring myself back to reality.

What the hell was that?

I stared and studied her expression as I realized she had not seen what I had. She breathed heavily as she raised the dull sword to my throat and claimed the win. I dropped my sword and lifted my hands in surrender as I watched her eyes swell with tears.

Jimmy and Mags were standing by the tree and watched nervously as I stood and steadied myself.

"You win," I agreed, rubbing my jaw where the bruise was already forming. I stood, dumbfounded as to what just happened, and walked over to the magic filled sword, handing it over to her. Realizing that whatever hell she was going through was personal, I knew she definitely needed this win more than me.

The four of us sat for the next few hours as we laughed about old myths that were surely nonsense and then of stories of our ancestors that made a little more sense. The afternoon sun was beginning to set as I watched Izzy fidgeting with her braids. I knew she was fighting her own demons inside, and I needed to be a gentleman like my father would want me to be.

I got up and walked over to her. "Can I ask what's in your sack?"

She inhaled sharply and turned to stare at me. "Nothing."

"Is there a broken stone in there?"

She glared back at me, shocked.

"I'm sorry if that scares you, but I think I had a vision or something. I saw it clear as day."

She inhaled, holding her breath as she slowly grabbed the bag and opened the top, reaching her hands in slowly and lifting out the exact same stone I had seen.

Exhaling as she closed her eyes and waited. There it was, shattered in two, revealing a fossilized dragon that I have only ever seen in books as a child. I gasped and went to reach for it. Izzy snatched her hands back and held it close to her chest while she began to cry.

"I broke it, I didn't mean to. My father is going to kill me. He thinks it will get his chaos magic back. I didn't mean to break it."

I froze, not expecting her to say anything more and slowly reached over to her and wrapped my arms around her. She just needed a better father to raise her. She has been through hell with that man. "Iz, I'm so sorry. Maybe we can fix it. When will your father be home?"

"He's probably waiting there for me now, arms crossed and tapping his foot." Her crying slowed as she wiped her snot onto her sleeve. "Do you really think you can fix it?"

"Well, not me alone. Maybe together we can mend it." I shrugged. "Here, let me see it."

She handed me the Jasper stone and watched carefully with hope filled eyes.

"Give me your hand." I reached for her and silently whispered to the gods, begging them to mend this broken worthless piece of stone and also to mend her broken heart. We each placed our palms on the stone as I whispered incantations that I'd heard my mother say many times before as she fixed broken toys.

Her and I stood as I said the words louder. Jimmy and Mags ran over to us as the stone began to have an ominous glow. We all stared in shock and then awe as it lifted into the air and spun in circles out of our reach.

Magic began to mend it while my forearm began to tingle. I looked down at it confused and tried to rub the tingling away. I watched as Izzy reached for hers and mimicked me.

Smartass.

The stone slowed from its axis and began to descend back down into my hands as I heard whispering from the gods tell me secrets that were surely not to be known. I looked at Izzy and the others and realized no one else heard the whispers.

"The immortality spell will work, and when it does, you need to find the broken one and mend her. She is destined for great things or evil. You must be the one to protect her from wrong. Do you understand? Without her, the magic world will not survive."

I stood astonished as I listened to the beautiful voice and watched as a sheer glimmering lady appeared in front of me, smiling. I looked around and realized everyone else and the field had vanished again, and it was just her and I standing in front of one another.

"You will have a heavy weight to carry with this one, but you must." Her lips pursed, and she seemed to be some sort of goddess, beyond beautiful and surely the purest of pure. She looked down at me and narrowed her eyes, no longer seeming pure but annoyed. *"Do you hear me, child?"*

"Yes," I whispered when I finally found my voice. *"Yes, I'm to find the broken one. Yes, you have my word."*

The world came spinning back to me as my brother grabbed my shoulder and examined me. "Who are you talking to?" He pulled my eyelids open wide and watched carefully. "I think Izzy gave you a head spin." He laughed as he slapped my back. "Alright, she's won. Give her the sword. We need to leave before the moon rises."

I nodded and watched Izzy carefully as I handed her the mended stone and the dragon's blood sword. "Here, you've won."

Izzy grabbed both the stone and sword before turning quickly and tugging Mags along with her. She came to a halt and turned back around. She ran back to me and leaned up, kissing me on my cheek. "Thank you," she whispered before running back to her sister.

I wiped my cheek as I shook my head in confusion over what the hell just happened. I rubbed my temples as I tried to memorize what the floating lady told me as we walked back home to our mother before the evils came out at night. I kept my eyes on my forearm and waited for something to appear where the tingling began. For a brief moment, I thought I saw the slight glimmer of a triangle, but nothing more happened, and the tingling stopped. Life continued on as if no connection had just been made.

"You coming?" Jimmy yelled ahead of me.

"Yeah, I'm coming," I yelled back, as I ran to catch up with him.

Isadora Cambridge

I ran inside and placed the mended stone where it belonged, smiling with relief that I would live to see another day. I grabbed the sword and hid it under my bed before running down the stairs to wash up for dinner. Father was late, and for that, I was thankful. Mother was waiting for me at the bottom of the stairs. Her expression told me she had a secret.

"We will not speak of any of this to your father. Understood?"

I looked up to her and watched as her face hardened. I swallowed hard and nodded.

"Run along now, and do yourself a favor—stay out of his room."

I slumped down, knowing that she knew. "I'm sorry."

"We have much to discuss."

Mags ran to the table and sat next to me, giggling like a child on cloud nine for getting to spend the afternoon with her stupid crush. She was glowing, though, and I laughed at her childish grin, happy for her.

"Please do not tell Father we were there."

"You were where?" Our father entered the room with the tone of voice that would make anyone lower into their seat.

"Oh, just down by the river."

"Still lying, I see, Syphon. Have you perfected your powers yet, or are you still trying to win on the battlefield for priceless metals?"

"Father, I can win. I can beat—"

"You can do nothing," he interrupted. "You must work harder to perfect your syphoning skills. I want my magic back, and only you can give it to me." He scoffed in disgust. "Since you were the one who stole it."

"Father, I didn't steal anything."

"Shut your mouth, you are the reason my magic was taken. The day you were born, you syphoned it right out of me. Now, all I have left are these weak mind tricks that do me no good anymore." He paced back and forth. "Power is what I had, and power is what I will get back when you learn to syphon from others."

"Dear," my mother said, "that is enough. Come on, little loves, let's go eat in the loft together. Your father is tired from his journey and needs his quiet now." Mother glared at him while lifting our plates to follow her. Mags and I walked behind her with our heads down as I heard him whisper under his breath.

"Worthless twins."

We sat in the loft with our mother, and the room became full of life again.

"Ugh, why does he even come back at all?"

"Isadora, don't say such things. He is still your father."

I huffed. "He is evil, even I can see that."

She exhaled slowly. "Your father is…" She inhaled and debated on her next words carefully. "Your father had so much power before your birth. To the point where any man, woman, or child would bow to him at the flick of his wrist. His mind tricks were simple compared to his strength of the chaos magic he's lost. He was both powerful and dangerous, and I have to admit that I was happy the day he lost his power." She swallowed hard and held her Labradorite stone necklace tight. "Recently, when he found that Jasper stone in the river, he began to slowly regain his chaos magic, and that worries me that he will become his powerful self again if he finds more objects."

"The Jasper stone is helping him?"

My mother nodded as she nervously twirled her necklace. "And that is why he has been gone so much lately. He is on the hunt for more magical objects. He believes each object is helping him regain his power."

She sighed. "He thinks the planet's alignment will help tap into his chaos."

I looked at Mags, then back at her and seemed to be the only one to notice she was hiding something from us.

I looked down at her iridescent Labradorite necklace and felt the guilt inside me as I knew that I broke father's hope by breaking that stone. I may have ruined it completely, and now I was keeping it a secret from my mother. She deserved to know the truth. I fidgeted with my braids as I decided it was better to let her in on my failure.

"Mother, that stone… I—"

My mother covered my mouth and shook her head, placing her stone under her garment against her chest. I stared back at her confused—it was not her Labradorite that I had meant at all.

"Shh. Do not speak it. He could be listening," she whispered.

My eyes widened as I realized the danger that could put me in.

"Stay away from him. He is becoming someone else entirely. Do you girls understand me?"

I nodded. Mags was already eating and not listening to a word that was being said. She slowed her chewing and looked back at our mother and nodded.

Mother knew my secret, and this whole conversation was meant for me. She leaned in closer to me and whispered, "One day, you will need to use your syphoning toward his darkness and bring out the light." She kissed my forehead and leaned back, lifting her plate of food and eating quietly.

My arm started to tingle again. I looked down and saw the shimmer of a symbol appear and then disappear again. Something in the world felt off. I excused myself and walked down the stairs and into the main room.

There he was, standing over the Jasper stone, holding onto it tight as it glowed between his hands.

I finally exhaled as I realized it wasn't completely ruined.

We had had that stone for over a month, and it had only glowed three times. The first day he brought it home and I snuck into his room to see it, the second in the field today when it mended, and now while he was holding it. There was something being activated inside of it, and it all started when I first touched it. Something drew me to the Jasper and I wanted it to be mine. The little tiny fossil it held inside was begging for me to protect it from him.

I watched closely as my father lifted it into the air and smiled in a way that didn't seem pleasant. I tiptoed back and tried to go back to my mother but was stopped without my physical doing and turned to face my father.

"Syphon, come here now." I could hear his voice in my head, but his lips didn't move. He pointed to me, and without my own doing, my legs moved toward him. My body reached his as his free hand touched my head, and a spiral of the past days and the stupid stone played over in my head. I looked up through the images as my father kept his eyes on me. My eyes widened as I realized what he was doing. He was rummaging in my head.

"Get off me. Mother, help me!" I yelled, as I tried to push back from him.

"Stop moving," he screamed, as he broke deeper into my memories. "You did something to this, and I want to see how."

I grabbed his arm and tried to syphon from him, only to have my forearm twisted in an unnatural way. A pain shot through my entire arm as my wrist became distorted, making me scream in pain. Making me look like a coward. Tears welled instantly as the image of the field appeared when Eric and I fought. My screaming continued, and just before he could see the next moment of the stone mending, my father's body was thrown back into the wall by a gust of wind, and my mother came to stand behind me breathing heavily.

"Do not touch her ever again," my mother yelled, as he got back up with rage filled eyes. "Little love, get your sister and go next door please."

"But, Mother," I cried, not wanting to leave her, cradling my wrist to my chest.

"I said, go," she yelled again, only this time I didn't hesitate. I guarded my tender wrist and ran upstairs to grab Mags, dragging her down the ladder with my good wrist and running next door to Oxana's. Mags stared back at me with horror filled eyes as I tried to open Oxana's door and failed while the pain radiated down my arm. Without hesitation, Mags pushed the door open, and we ran in. Oxana sat at her table drinking her herbs. She looked up from her mug and smiled until she saw the tears flowing down my cheeks. I tried to hide them, but the pain was excruciating. Her smile flipped, and her nostrils flared as I watched her pupils flicker with rage.

"Come sit, girls." She pointed to the table and examined my wrist before standing to grab two more mugs. "Let's fix that." She handed me a tea of some sort. "Drink this." I did as told with a shaky hand, and immediately the pain that was radiating in my wrist started to subside.

I stared back at her in wonder and examined my bone shifting under my skin. Part of me wanted to vomit, but the pain was becoming less, and another part of me wanted to cry with tears of joy. I nodded and watched my wrist become straight again with a quick '*pop*'.

"Good," she said. "Now let me make you some warm milk and honey. It'll help you both sleep easy tonight."

I twisted my wrist around and was astonished by the easy movement and that pain was completely gone. Mags looked like she was ready to pass out, which made me want to laugh, considering she was the healer of the two of us. She would surely have to heal many brutal injuries in the future.

I sniffled and wiped my tears away, nodding as I replayed the last few moments in my head. "Thank you, Oxana."

"You two are always welcome here, day or night." She winked as she poured the mixture.

My head swarmed with thoughts from earlier. I wanted to know more. I needed answers of what my father was capable of.

"Mags, how about you go in the next room and count the stars? I will meet you there in a few minutes," I whispered.

She swallowed and then smiled as she gladly walked away.

"What do you know of my father's past?" I asked Oxana when Mags was out of earshot.

Oxana inhaled slowly and half smiled. "Oh, child, that is not for me to discuss. Lady Cambridge will tell you when she is ready."

"Please, she tries to shelter us from all evil, but I know my father isn't good."

She smirked. "You are beyond your years. Very wise, like your mother." She exhaled and studied my eager expression. "Your father became obsessed with power before you two were born. To the point where he began to sacrifice other witches to consume their strength with a Hildisvini dagger." She looked toward the door at the crashing going on next door in our home. "Your mother and I had planned on running from him, but then you two were born, and his magic stopped. Your mother was able to give the pagan family the dagger back. Problem solved. His head games stopped altogether for a little while. Everything became more peaceful." She smiled. "You two saved us from his wrath of wanting to watch the world burn, and he must never get that power back."

"But then his head games started again…"

She nodded. "But those have been weak, until tonight it seems. They are nothing as powerful as his chaos magic was, though."

I shook my head. "Why now?"

She shrugged. "He thinks those planets aligning will give him a celestial event that will help him get his magic back. He has been working on a plan, and his secrecy is what scares me. Whatever he has planned… it can't be good."

"He wants to hold the world, our world, in his palm and watch it burn… Doesn't he?"

Oxana frowned. "I hope not, but I believe you are correct."

I sat wide eyed, never hearing that part of the story before and not expecting Oxana to be the one to confirm it. "How could my mother stay with him?"

She laughed. "It was an arranged marriage to combine the lands. It was a duty that your mother has surely fulfilled ten times over." She shrugged. "Now drink up, and let's get you to bed. I will head over and check on Lady Cambridge."

"Thank you." I lifted the mug and chugged the milk quickly until there wasn't a drop left.

Oxana nodded and kissed me on the forehead before heading to our broken home. I ran to the window, wiping the lingering drink from my mouth, to watch her wrath. I stood shocked when Oxana blew the door open with a flick of her wrist. I wasn't sure if it was just the milk making me hallucinate, but I swore I saw scales appear along her arms and neck as she called upon the water of the river to flow along her scaly claws as she walked into our home ready for battle.

I quickly jumped down from the ledge and shook my head. Trying to not over imagine what would happen next, I walked in the room and saw Mags, quietly deciding not to tell her of what happened. She was so innocent and sweet. She didn't need any of the ugly from this world or any world. I needed to protect her from evil.

All evil.

I needed to be the one to keep her safe.

"Forty-four and two shooting stars. Hurry and make a wish. One for you, and one for me." She smiled as I laid down next to her in the open roof room and grabbed the fur to keep us warm under the stars.

"I wish—"

"Shhh." She grabbed my lips and sealed them. "You can't tell me, or it won't work."

I laughed as she unleashed my lips. "You and your superstitions."

I grabbed her hand with my mended wrist and held it close to me for a few minutes before I closed my eyes. "Love you, Mags," I whispered to her and waited for a response. Her silence made me realize she was sound asleep, and I smiled at her light snoring. "I wish for you to have a full life of love and happiness forever and forever."

Chapter 4
Eric Greystone

It had been a few weeks since the field fight with Izzy, but word had it that she was alive and her father never found out about the breakage of that stone. For her sake, I was grateful. I hoped that one day she would use that dragon's blood sword on her father and slice his head off. Take him out of this world for good.

I could hear my mother talking with Oxana and Lady Cambridge in the next room, and I crept close to the doorway to listen. I could hear the tone shift from fear to anger as Lady Cambridge spoke ill of Ragnar.

"I could take him myself. I just don't want him to destroy the lands and our people before I can contain him," Lady Cambridge said.

"Your parents paired you with him to do just that. You were strong enough. Had only you not fallen pregnant with his children, then he would have already been concealed."

I heard Lady Cambridge sniffle. "Evil or not, he was still their father. But now, he has taken things too far. He broke Izzy's wrist a few weeks ago, and he knows the Jasper stone is now activated. He will manipulate her into bringing his chaos magic back into this world."

I heard the sobs begin, and I felt guilty listening in on information that was not meant for my ears.

"Oh, dear, come here." my mother's voice chimed in, as I heard the shuffle of movement, and I assumed she grabbed Lady Cambridge for comfort. "We will not let him get into their heads. No matter what, we will protect them from his evil ways."

"I should've killed him years ago." she sobbed. "It's what my parents sent me to him for. I was to end his wrath before he ever had children."

"He tricked you, Nicola. You were to wed him and then slit his throat that same night. How would you have known his true mind power until he forced himself upon you?"

"I know." Lady Cambridge cried harder.

"Luckily, that gave us nine months of planning to get his magic out of him the day the girls were born," Oxana said.

"Does he know anything yet? About where you kept it?" my mother asked. I waited for her response but heard nothing. "Well, that's good."

Kept what?

I leaned in a little closer, but as the weight of my body slipped, I fell into the doorway, exposing myself to their secrets.

"Eric Frey Greystone, I swear, I will drag you by the ears the next time you impose on others' conversations."

I jumped up, fear filling my face. "I'm so sorry. I didn't mean to." I cleared my throat and prayed to live.

I watched as Lady Cambridge wiped her tears, and the women laughed as my vulnerable young-self stood up and straightened my shirt.

My mother waved for me to come over to her, still chuckling at my own stupidity. I never felt more like a coward under my mother's wrath. I shyly walked to her and knelt down next to her, ashamed that I had been caught and irritated that I didn't hear more secrets that were surely forbidden from me for too many reasons.

She leaned over and whispered, "You make sure that you keep those twins close to you. They will both need your protection one day, and you will soon enough be immortal to do so. Do you understand me?"

I felt the weight of the world get heavier on my shoulders as the duty of protecting others was added. Until the thought of me protecting Izzy made me want to laugh. She had enough sword fighting in her that she could protect herself and her sister. She didn't need me at all.

But I nodded to obey my mother, then closed my eyes so she couldn't see them roll.

"Eric, you know that one day you and my daughter are destined to marry and join the remaining lands as one. It is your duty to do so," Lady Cambridge spoke.

"But I am not the oldest, my broth—"

"No, it will be you. Jimmy has already spoken for Margaret. He is to claim her after the immortality ceremony. We need the lands bonded as strongly as possible for any future battles to come."

I nodded, pissed off, but understood that our lands becoming one was more important. A duty that was now both up to my brother and me to keep. Plus, I would never let a woman get in my way of my travels. I would wed her, give myself an heir, and continue to travel the lands and sea, claiming the lands until the name Greystone roared throughout the world.

"Yes, ma'am."

I held my jaw tight so as to not say another word. Besides, I could never love Izzy in that way. She was my *friend*. I would protect her, but no woman would have my heart. Love was for the weak. A mere distraction to power. Too many warriors have been killed over the stupid word.

Why did I need a woman in my life anyway? Couldn't I just be Eric the Great, the conqueror of lands, a warrior?

I waited to be dismissed so they could continue to talk in private.

I tiptoed out of the room as quickly as possible before they added more to my list of duties and grabbed my satchel to run for the field. I needed my thinking space and that was the last of the land that was not filled with homes and trades. I ran quickly and I prayed that I would be alone there. I broke through the last of the trees and ran into the clearing. Panting as I tried to catch my breath, I laid down on the field and stared up at the blue sky. I could hear the river rushing in the distance and tried to let my mind focus on the tranquility of peace and quiet.

"What did you find out?"

I jumped as Izzy stood over me, arms crossed with her snarky attitude.

"Woah, what the hell?" Annoyed, I sat up and tried to contain my own fear at being caught off guard. I hadn't even heard her footsteps.

"Well?" She sat down next to me and waited. "You were spying on them, weren't you? I saw you through the window, you had the best earshot."

I laughed as she assumed what I was doing. I shook my head. "Nope."

"You liar. Tell me what they were saying about my father."

I jumped up and paced back and forth, debating on what needed to be said and what I could keep to myself. "Just that your father broke your wrist."

She huffed as she stood up and charged her palm with a fireball before releasing the energy across the field as she tossed it with her now mended wrist. "Doesn't look broken to me." She smirked as she whispered, "Ignis," and lit her palm with another one and brought it closer for me to examine.

"Well, good." I lifted my palm and hovered it over hers, "Aqua," letting water smother her fire. "You need to stay away from him."

She laughed. "Easier said than done."

"I'm serious, Izzy. He's planning something, and I don't want to have to save you."

She scoffed. "*You* save me? Please, I can save myself. I'm not afraid of him."

"Well, you should be. He's mind melding again, and next thing you know, he will be destroying the lands and killing us all."

Her eyes met mine, and for the first time, I saw her— her fear of him. She shook her head and fidgeted with her braids.

"Just don't let him in your head, okay?"

She nodded before walking away. Whatever I said must've hit a nerve because she looked defeated. I shook my head and laid back down, letting the warmth and rustling of the light wind put me to sleep.

Isadora Cambridge

"Was my mother really at their home telling them about my father's actions? That made me look like a coward and weak." I scoffed to myself.

I didn't like that at all. I grabbed a branch from the tree and snapped it in half, whipping it around like a sword.

"I am Isadora Cambridge, and I am the champion of the lands. Bow to me, or feel my father's wrath." I giggled to myself as I walked back to our home with the stick in hand. Mags stayed back with our mother at the Greystone land, and I smiled, knowing that I could get some peace and quiet at home for once.

I walked into our home and went straight to my bed, looking up at the cracks through the roof where I could stargaze at night when it was dry. I sat up and reached under my bed for the dragon's blood sword to examine before *his* voice ruined my peace.

"Syphon, get out here, now."

I groaned as I heard my father's voice boom through the hall.

Damn it.

He was supposed to be away today.

I sat up and inched my way toward him, hearing my mother's warning in the back of my head. *Stay away from him.*

"Yes, Father?"

He was sitting on the stairs with the Jasper stone in his hand, broken in two pieces. I gasped when I saw the stone split again and waited for his wrath.

"I'm sorry—"

"I did it." He stood up and smiled, holding a piece in each hand. "I was able to get a fraction of the magic from here. Come here, come try and syphon from me. See what you feel."

I walked over slowly and obliged.

I started to pull and froze when I felt a small tingle hit my fingertips. I retracted my hand too quickly out of fear. His smile met my eyes as I stepped away from him.

"See, now you're going to help me get the full magic from inside this and more objects like these." He raised the two halves in the air with demand.

I stepped further back and rubbed the wrist that he had hurt. He saw me wince as I relived the moment of betrayal.

"Oh, my sweetest Isadora, I did not know my own strength. I must've had my magic coming through without knowing it. I would never hurt you intentionally."

"But you did," I said while I backed away from him, getting ready to run for the field, far away from him.

42

His sly smile crossed his face as his words grew louder, though his lips stayed motionless.

I froze in shock, hearing him clear as day. My stomach began to spiral as bile tried to escape.

"Your wrist was never broken, and you want to help me get more objects to get my magic back because you believe that I am very deserving of it, and you love me, and our bond is unbreakable."

I stared back at my father, confused, but then I nodded as the words became true in my head.

My father *was* a sweet man. His poor soul, to have had his chaos magic taken from him because of my birth. It was truly cruel. I looked down at my wrist and forgot why I had been holding it in the first place. My mind felt lighter, as if it was not firing on its own and I didn't have to do anything to help it. *Weightless.* I felt happy and loved. I looked up at my father and smiled before skipping over to him and admiring the two halves of the Jasper stone and examined the fossil between them. I was in such distress when it broke that I never even examined it close enough to notice. I gasped when I noticed the baby bones and the wings that arched over the top. It was not a stone at all. It was a dragon's egg made of Jasper that had fossilized itself—a baby dragon forever embedded inside it.

"Is that a dragon's egg?" My gaze would not break from the innocent little creature inside.

"It was at one point, twin dragons to be exact. They shared the egg, and now it is the key to giving me my magic back." He patted my back and turned me toward him. "This will be our little secret. There must be more of them. We will search for more in the river."

I nodded, wanting to help him heal himself.

A strange twinge in my stomach started to make me feel nauseous, but something told me I had to help him. That he deserved his power again. I had stolen it from him when I was born, and now I needed to help get it back.

"Why don't you have Mags heal you? She could use her po—"

"She is weak, a waste of space."

I stood shocked as the door opened. My mother and Mags walked back in. My mother's eyes bulged as she ran to me and pulled me away from him.

"Get away from her," she sneered.

"Mother, stop. He didn't do any—"

"She's fine," my father spat back.

My mother grabbed my wrist and lifted it in front of my face. "He broke this, and now you want to be his friend?"

I stood, confused, shaking my head.

My wrist had never been broken before. No bones in my body had ever snapped. Cuts and bruises, sure. But never anything that would not heal itself quickly.

Was she beginning to go mad?

"It's not broken."

"Yes, thanks to Oxana."

My father took a step closer toward us and froze as my mother raised her palms in front of him with fire.

"I said, stay away from them. Don't make me hurt you."

He smirked as he waved his magicless hands in defense, mocking her.

"Protect me."

A feeling inside me burned. A wave of nausea took over me. I didn't want my mother to hurt him—he was my father and he was a good man. I jumped in between them and brought flames to my palms to protect him.

"Don't hurt him."

"Isadora Ember Cambridge, get away—"

I let the flames grow as anger started to fill me. "I said, don't." Releasing a flame in the direction of my loved ones, I watched it hit the wall next to them as they dodged my uncontrolled anger.

My mother dropped her palms and let the flames extinguish before looking back at me with saddened eyes. "You are too young for any of this." She grabbed her Labradorite necklace and my sister's hand before running back outside. I lowered my palms and stared at them with even my own disbelief. Something did not *feel* right.

"Good, child. You did good." My father walked up behind me, cheering for me. The admiration he was giving me was what I had been looking for since the day I was born. I had finally done something right in his eyes, even though my stomach was twisting and telling me to run to my mother.

"I, uh, I—"

"You did good." He nodded toward the door and shook his head. "Your mother doesn't understand. With my magic back, I can do so much more. You and I can rule this entire earth and do as we please. The power I had was unstoppable. I can create new lands and make the river flow where I want to again. I was a god, and I will be again." His grin made me want to crawl out of my skin. "You will help me be great again."

Power was not something that I cared about. I wanted my family to be whole. I wanted my father to love me, and for some reason, a little part inside of me, after this night, I thought he might actually care about me. I wasn't sure what had changed, but deep down, I was happy that I had made him proud for once.

"Now let's get back to work, starting with that sister of yours."

My heart beat faster as I admired my father's bond with me talking instead of yelling, and whatever we were planning had to be for the greater good of getting his power back so he could be happy and our family could be whole again. I looked up to him and nodded as he opened his family's grimoire and started to look at ingredients that I had never heard of. Whatever black henbane was did not seem like it was going to be for the greater good, and my mind began to spin again while trying to put the pieces together.

"You will be stronger once you consume her magic," his voice sneered, sending a shiver down my spine.

"Who's?" I asked.

"Your sister's. She's useless to us."

My eyes widened as I tried to understand. "Father, I can't take her magic. It will break our bond. I will no longer have my lifeline to keep me alive. I can't do that. It could kill her."

"Exactly. Twins are not natural. Only *you* were meant to be born. She stole your full potential of magic—and mine—and we need it back."

I stepped back, afraid of his crazy thoughts, and shook my head. Something was off. I would never hurt my sister. *Ever.*

"No," I said sternly and raised my palms in anger, letting them ignite against him now.

My father's eyes bulged as he looked up from his studies and smirked. His laugh started and echoed throughout our home. "Stupid child. If you think you can beat me… " He laughed again. "Don't make me do it again, Syphon."

I glared at him, confused, but stood my ground. "I will not hurt my sister."

"Fine." His smirk widened as his voice echoed in my head while his lips never moved.

"Your sister wants you to take her magic. It's killing her from the inside. A poison, so to speak. You need to help her and remove it. It's the only way. You must syphon her magic to save her soul from the damned."

My body froze as I stared at my palms, extinguishing the flames.

"Father, is Mags sick?"

He nodded with saddened eyes.

"I think I know how to fix her." I closed my palms and felt my syphoning tingle under my skin.

"Good." He smiled.

"I need to step outside and get some air. I'm starting to feel unwell."

"Okay, my sweet Isadora. I'll get the ingredients list started."

I nodded and walked outside, feeling in a daze. My head felt heavy, like smog was brewing inside my thoughts. Something didn't feel right, but I couldn't place where the strange feeling was stemming from. The world was going crazy. I looked up and watched as the planets began to align. I watched as the far away worlds became closer to one another. I shook my head at how legends said that when the planets finally aligned with the moon, our world would either thrive or go mad. I was sure it was only a myth, but the way I feel right now and with Mags being very sick, it must be true.

My mother tore me back into reality as she yanked me and shook me hard. "Izzy, wake up. Whatever trance he's got you in, you need to wake up."

The entire world was spinning as she shook me hard. I watched as the planets became blurry, and finally my head started to clear. "Geez, I'm awake, Mother. Let me go," I snapped.

She released her grip and examined me closely.

"What did he say to you?" she frantically asked. "What has he done?"

"Mother, I'm fine. Mags is sick, and I need to heal her. He's trying to help her." I grunted in annoyance.

My mother's eyes bulged as she gasped. Holding her hand over her mouth, tears started to form. "No, no, no. Izzy, you must never syphon from your twin—ever. That is uncharted territory, and if you attempt it, the universe could implode. Or worse, you could kill her."

I huffed as she said the words. "I would never hurt my sister. It will only heal her."

"No, child. It will quite do the opposite." She grabbed me fiercely, pinching my arms too tight, making me face her directly. "Promise me you will never do that to her. Your father is messing with your head."

"You're hurting me," I squirmed under her grasp. "He would never do that to me. He loves me, and I love my sister. I would never hurt her. Ever." I tried to escape her hold. "Please, let me go. She's my best friend."

She stared at me with such concern that it made me uncomfortable. "Okay… thank the Goddesses," she said, as she released me, putting her hand at my back and pushing me along to Oxana's home. She sealed the door behind us as we stepped inside. I stood in the middle of the room, confused about why she was so scared and why Oxana had literal fire in her eyes as she looked out of her window back at our house. I swear I could see literal smoke coming from her nostrils as I walked past her. I shook my head and walked over to Mags. I smiled when I laid down next to her and started counting the stars with her.

"What took you so long?" she asked.

"Father was proud of me for the first time. Can you believe it?" I smiled as she sat up and looked down at me.

"Proud of you for what?" She stared back in confusion.

"I, uh, I… don't really remember." The images of the night started to blur together, and pieces of the last few hours became unclear as to what was real and what wasn't.

Had I been dreaming?

Why don't I remember what I was doing?

Why was he proud of me?

I looked up to Mags and shook my head. "I don't think I feel so well. I'm going to close my eyes for a bit. I love you, Mags."

She watched me intently as I turned my body away from her. "Love you too."

And before I knew it, my eyes slammed shut, and my brain needed as much sleep as possible. It felt like it was rerouting roots down different paths, and I couldn't seem to figure out why. Sleep would cure me. Sleep was all I needed to be myself again.

At least, I hoped so.

Chapter 6
Eric Greystone

The stars looked mesmerizing as I counted each one and hoped that one day I could see more of this world than just my own lands. The planets were moving closer each night, which made me feel that something was happening, and I wasn't sure if it was something I wanted.

I heard the door open, then whispers coming from down below. I creeped out of my bed and walked to the open staircase to peer down, trying to be more discreet than my earlier failed attempt at stealth.

I listened and watched as Oxana argued with my mother over Ragnar and his power again. My mother turned and walked into the kitchen with Oxana following. I thought I had been out of sight until Oxana stopped and turned to look back up at me. She winked and waved her hand in a motion, inviting me in to listen. At least, I assumed. I tiptoed my way down the stairs as Jimmy creeped out of his room and began to follow me.

He waved to get my attention, and I turned around and shushed him, motioning for him to follow me. I whispered, "Oxana is here," and nodded toward the kitchen as we made our way to the back entrance of the room and listened.

"Is your husband back yet?" Oxana asked.

"No, he's been delayed down the river. I received a letter a few days ago."

"We don't have time to wait." Oxana raised her voice. "He's begun to rummage in Izzy's head… that poor child." She shook her head. "All of the gods know how fragile that one is."

I heard my mother gasp. "She's so young." Her tongue tsked. "I can't do the immortality spell yet. I need my husband. He has the rune stone with the spell we need, and the boys should really be a little older. They're still learning their own magic. I can't give them another task to kill Ragnar."

I heard the chair skid across the ground as Oxana huffed. "We definitely don't have years."

I jumped as my brother bumped into me. I turned around quickly and glared. His eyes showed how he was frightened as we both processed what our future mission was.

Kill Izzy's father? I mean, I'd killed many others in battle. But this was different. I knew the face of the man they wanted killed and by *my* doing, I knew who his family was.

I swallowed hard.

My mother's voice spoke sternly. "You don't think I know what I have to do? I'm risking my own children to defeat a monster. I know it needs to be done, but they are my children." She sniffled. "We all know Ragnar's chaos magic is coming to the surface again. I can see the fire growing behind his eyes and we all know that he can not get it back. He almost destroyed our lands twelve years ago— We were nearing the brink of destruction. He was ready to kill everyone that had any form of magic. He wanted to be the only one left with power. I mean, hell… he even killed his own mother to obtain that dark magic that we call chaos. To sacrifice your most loved person in the world just to obtain a poisonous magic that embeds itself into your soul and eats away at you like a disease… that type of magic can destroy any world."

We stood speechless.

Oxana broke the silence after a long exhale. "I understand why you are hesitant and I know your heart is in the right place. Just do the spell now, and your boys will continue to age until maturity any way. Use it as a failsafe in case Ragnar comes for them when word spreads that your boys can kill him. And word will spread."

The room became silent for a moment

"They don't even know how. We don't even know if the dagger to the heart will work," my mother finally spoke.

"Nicola is leaving something out, an ingredient or something." Oxana huffed. "I will find out."

There was a long pause, and I briefly debated on walking away.

"Okay, I'll do it. In two days. The night the planets finish aligning. We can harvest power from the celestial event. Hopefully, their father will be back with the runestone spell by then." It was my mother who spoke softly. "But, you better jump in when Ragnar comes. My boys will need your claws."

"I will be there every step of the way." Oxana promised.

"I will talk to them tonight. I will explain everything." My mother promised.

I stepped back and walked to the window, looking up at how the planets were already closer than I liked.

"Only two days?" I said under my breath. "Dooming me to live an eternity without my loved ones." I shook my head and ran outside to catch my breath, and my brother followed.

"This is horseshit," I yelled when he reached me. Breathing heavily, my irritation grew knowing that I had any duty at all at my young age. I didn't want any of this. I just wanted to explore the lands on my own.

"Hey, it'll be alright." Jimmy grabbed me and pulled me in closer to him. "At least we will be able to live forever."

I huffed. "I don't want that. Have you even thought about what immortality means?"

"Yeah, it means we can't be killed."

I shoved his shoulder. "It means that everyone we love will age and die, and we will still be alive. What kind of sick torture is that? Any womanly love we have, they will age and die. Mags will age and die. And what of our little sister waiting for us in Valhalla? Will we ever see her again?"

He became silent as he finally understood the true consequences.

"Yeah, doesn't sound so fun anymore, does it?" I said, shaking my head.

He exhaled slowly. "I guess I was only thinking about the next few years being indestructible. I hadn't thought about the truth of forever yet."

I walked toward the wooden cart of hides and sat at the edge of it, leaning back against tomorrow's profits. Jimmy walked over and sat with me.

"Did you hear about Izzy?" I asked and shook my head, irritated. "If her father is manipulating her, then we need to help save her. I don't want her mind so melted that I have to marry a cuckoo in the next few years." I laughed, trying to lighten the news.

He laughed too. "We can save her and Mags. Let's take them and run away. Start over fresh."

"I'm not leaving home with Ragnar still causing chaos on our lands. Our parents are here."

Jimmy nodded. "I was kidding."

I sat up quickly and stared down at him. "But maybe you and Mags should run. Grow old together. I know the sword is not your strong suit. I'm sure I can handle Ragnar myself. Besides, you might just get in the way of me having to save you."

He sat up and glared at me.

"I'm not leaving you. We're family, and family is forever."

I rolled my eyes. "Okay, Mother."

He laughed. "Well, she's right."

"Yeah, yeah." I inhaled sharply. "I'm serious, though. Jimmy, if things don't go as planned, then you and Mags need to take off at dragon's speed. Promise me you will. I can find you when it's all over." I sighed heavily. "Live a long life and make gross little goblins and ghouls, just name one after me. You know, for my legacy."

He huffed as he shook his head. "It's not going to come to that."

"It very well might."

We sat in silence before he finally spoke.

"You know what I miss?"

"What's that?"

"The middle." He smiled.

I turned and laughed. "The land of make believe to run from our childish problems."

He shrugged. "I don't know… It was always fun and safe. I've never been able to open my mind enough to get there, like you can."

I sat quietly, not wanting him to know the real reason I made it was to live alone peacefully in it. Escape from the fate of immortality and wars. It was a safe space for me to clear my head, but it was stupid. A world like ours, only empty of people. Who would actually want that?

The front door of our home opened as Oxana walked outside and headed straight for us. I watched her amulet bounce off her chest as she made her way over.

"You better have been listening. I'm done letting your mother sugar coat things." She spat as she grabbed my arm and pulled me up from my seat, breathing heavily in front of me. "Did you hear me, Eric? You and your brother need to kill Ragnar and fast. Izzy is going to try and kill her sister." She exhaled heavily. "Consuming one's magic is dark and will damn us all for generations to come, if we even get that much time."

My eyes bulged as I looked back at Jimmy, who had steam blowing from his ears and a glare that could kill anyone that would stand in his way. He stood up and ripped my arm from Oxana.

"When?" he growled. For the first time, he seemed like the defensive older brother he was supposed to be.

Oxana shook her head. "Soon." She sat and rubbed her temples. "I am trying to keep you all safe. I am not strong enough to take on Ragnar on my own. He can get in my head." She looked up and examined me. "Maybe he hasn't gotten to you two."

"Mind manipulation only works on the weak." I puffed out my chest and felt strong for a brief second until Oxana's hand came across and slapped my face.

"This is serious." She glared at me.

"I am being serious. I doubt he can do it to me. I won't let him."

"Watch your tongue. I am far from weak, and it works on me."

I realized her irritation and looked down into the dirt. "I'm sorry."

"Listen to me. In two days, your mother will perform the immortality spell, and you two need to go after Ragnar that same night. If Izzy kills her sister, there will be consequences that no one will want to pay. Our elemental magic will change, and it won't be good. Do you understand me?"

I looked at Jimmy, who was still fuming. We both looked back at Oxana and nodded silently.

She stood up and smiled. "Good, the girls are staying at my home tonight, in case you need to see for yourself." She walked away before anything more could be said.

"I'm going to check on Izzy." I jumped up and straightened my shirt before marching toward Oxana's home to check on the twins. I knew I couldn't barge into it, but I at least needed to see if she was still standing her ground like the little warrior that she was.

The ghostlike woman's voice haunted me as I decided that Izzy had to be the broken one.

"Boys," our mother yelled from the doorway, searching for us in the dark. "Boys, come on in, we need to talk."

We both looked back toward the direction of her voice and then Jimmy turned back toward me. "We will talk to mother later, I'm coming with you." He grabbed my arm. "If he's hurting them…"

I nodded. "We save them."

So, there it was. A mutual agreement to be noble heroes.

He spit in his hand and held it out, waiting for our fate to be sealed. "Love you, brother."

"Always."

Isadora Cambridge

"Psst," a man's voice whispered. "Hey, come here."

I opened my eyes and looked around the room, listening intently. Debating if I was still dreaming, I looked over at Mags who was still sleeping soundly. The home was quiet. I peered toward the window and froze at a figure standing in the dark. They seemed to be motioning me over. I lifted my palms and whispered, "Ignis," as I let the flame form into an orb and let the fear turn to rage as I charged my palm, letting the flame grow, lighting it the entire room. I let my legs unthaw and slowly walked toward the window. The fire ignited Eric's face as he tried to hide his laughter. Then Jimmy was standing behind him, smirking.

"Stupid boys." I sneered and extinguished the flame before walking outside to meet them. "What do you want?"

Eric looked me up and down. "Are you okay?" He looked next door at my home and back at me. "I heard you may have had a rough night with your father."

I shook my head. "I'm fine." I stepped back and leaned against Oxana's house and waited.

"Oxana seemed to think differently," Jimmy added and looked back in the window, seeing Mags sleeping on the floor. "Is she okay?"

I stared back at them, confused, and then felt saddened. "She's sick. But my father said I can heal her." I nodded with confidence.

"Izzy, you are *not* a healer."

I pushed off the side of the home and shoved him. "You have always hated me. Will I never be enough for you?"

Eric grounded his feet and stepped back in place, eyes wide. "Iz… It's not that." I watched as he struggled with his words. He shook his head and groaned. "Come on, wake up Mags, and let's go explore the cave by the field."

I didn't know what he was thinking about, but I hoped that whatever it was, he would stick by my side as a friend until we could both grow older and get away from this place in one piece. Truly, besides Mags, he was the only other friend that I had. Whether he liked it or not.

We made our way up the rocky hill and climbed through the bluffs, letting the stones take their place on the earth as they fell beneath us. A thousand years from now we would be gone and another set of feet would be exploring these lands, the lands of our families that, with the use of magic and power, created the entire Cambridge/Greystone land for our people.

We didn't deserve it, though. The bluffs never should've been split in half like it was to create what we stand on today. My father decided to ruin the land before we were born, but I guessed other families were happy to have space to call home. As of late, we had not been invaded by any others, and we hoped that the stories of my father's power would keep everyone away from here.

"What are you thinking about?" Eric asked, grabbing my torso and pulling me into him. Every instinct in my body felt like I needed to pull away from him. I didn't *need* a man to take care of me. I was a strong warrior, and I didn't need him to think that I was a prized possession. Whether our families wanted us to marry and have heirs or not, I was *not* his.

"Don't touch me." I grabbed his arm and threw it off me.

He stopped walking and waited. "Iz, I didn't mean anything by it."

I felt my cheeks flush as my own embarrassment rose. I felt as if I had had enough men torture me and my own head, and Eric needed to know that he was my friend and that was all he would ever be to me. I didn't want love, and I surely didn't want his hands on me.

Mags and Jimmy were oblivious as they walked ahead, hand in hand, and giggled like stupid love birds that made me want to vomit.

Eric followed my stare and laughed. "I was not trying to hold your hand." He dropped to the edge of the field and laid back with a bellowing laugh. "I… was… trying… to clear… your head," he answered in between trying to catch his breath.

I sneered before finally realizing he was more like me than I thought. I exhaled heavily and began to laugh with him.

"I'm sorry," I whispered once I caught my own breath. "My father is such an ass. I just don't want to end up like my mother. In a situation she can't get away from. She doesn't say it, but she is miserable." I exhaled heavily. The more I thought about my father, the more I felt a strange warning to keep my distance. It was like, the further away from my home I was, the better I felt. I could swear that my father's madness was sickening our whole home and poisoning me from within, but then again, he's my father and I should be able to love him. My emotions felt torn in each direction today.

He sat up and wiped his eyes. He stared back at me and shook his head. "For one, I am nothing like your father. And two, I would never hurt you. You are my friend, and I will always protect you as best I can."

"You protect me?" I laughed and shoved his forearm, making him fall back onto the grass. He laughed as he stared up at the night sky.

"Eric," I whispered, debating if I actually wanted him to hear me or not.

He sat back up and waited.

"Do you think I am a bad person?" The words left my mouth before I had even decided if I wanted to know his truths.

His brows furrowed as he cautiously raised his hand in the air and slowly, gently put it on my shoulder, waiting for my recoil or possibly for me to burst into flames and sear him. He smirked when it finally touched my skin undamaged.

He shook my shoulder in reassurance and smiled. "Izzy Cambridge, I think you are incredibly brilliant, a strong warrior with a hell of a right hook, and that you are a savvy syphon who can do just about anything you put your mind to. I think you are beautiful both inside and out." He swallowed hard. "I think you got dealt a shitty hand of trades when it comes to who your father is, and I think he will try anything he can to ruin you, but I promise you, on this starry night and forward, that I will protect you from his evil. Every bit of chaos he has in him will not reach the surface of your heart while I am with you."

My eyes widened as his words seemed to melt the ice I had held close around my heart for too many years that a child should not have to hold. I felt my eyes begin to tear up at the inner corner, and for the first time, I let them fall happily without trying to hold them inside.

"A simple '*no*' would have sufficed." I smiled as he shrugged his shoulders.

"Someone needed to tell you." He winked and stood up, reaching for my hand. "Come on, the cave is waiting for us."

I grabbed his hand, and before I knew it, I wrapped my arms around his neck and let him pull me in tight for a hug.

"Thank you," I whispered and turned to kiss his cheek.

I smiled when I felt his entire body tense and his cheek turned to fire itself. I let him go and continued to walk as he stood back in place and lifted his hand to his cheek, smiling.

I didn't want a husband right now. But maybe in the future he could be a good one to keep close to me.

Chapter 8
Eric Greystone

My cheek burned with fire, and for the first time, it wasn't caused by true flames. I felt weak, and I didn't like feeling off guard.

Love was the one thing that I knew I could never have because love was pain and love was a distraction to winning wars.

No one that fought for love has ever won.

I wiped my cheek and shook my head before catching up to Izzy as we made our way to the cave in silence. I knew it was a moment that we would never talk about again. And for that, I was happy. It was our little secret, and we would leave it at that.

Jimmy and Mags were already in the cave. My brother had a chisel and was already writing his runes onto the walls of the rugged cave. I watched as he wrote his name and then added Mags' underneath. She blushed crimson red as he finished it.

I rolled my eyes and smirked.

Mags came over by Izzy like the child that she was and begged her. "Please, Iz, open the sky in here. It's my favorite part." She jumped up and down as Izzy walked to the walls of the cave and placed her hand on the surface. An ember glow began to form under her hand as the entire cave trembled slightly. I leaned against the opposite wall and looked up, waiting to see her tricks. Izzy closed her eyes, and the focus became stronger as the rumble of the ceiling disappeared and the starry night appeared above us, deep blue with speckled white filling the sky. I looked back at Izzy as she let go of the wall and inhaled heavily, catching her breath.

"I love it, thank you." Mags hugged her tight and ran back to my brother and pointed to the sky in awe.

I walked over to Izzy and grabbed her trembling hand. "Does that hurt you? To syphon?"

She pulled her hand away and hid it behind her back, shaking her head.

"'Course not."

I rolled my sleeve and laid out my forearm in front of her. "Here, syphon from me."

She shook her head. "I'm fine."

I grabbed her hand and wrapped her fingers around my forearm, not letting her release me. "I can stand here all night."

Her eyes met mine as she nodded. "Fine, just a little, though."

I nodded. "Deal."

I could feel the tingle of syphoning taking slowly from me but not enough to weaken. Her cheeks began to glow a little redder and she seemed to be more like herself again. I froze as my body tensed. Izzy and my surroundings disappeared as my forearm began to glow with two triangles interlocking.

When I looked back up everyone was gone except for the ghostly lady's face that had been haunting my mind. Her words to protect the broken one were living in my head daily.

I gasped as I turned around and realized it was just her and I.

"Okay, lady, who are you? And what do you want?"

She smiled softly and shook her head. *"It doesn't matter who I am. What matters is that you destroy my son before he breaks your world."*

I stood in shock with a confused look.

She hovered closer to me and surrounded me with her presence. Her voice was as gentle as a whisper—a dream that I could not wake from.

"Your son?" As soon as the words left my mouth, I gasped. *"You are Ragnar's mother."* I swallowed hard. *"He... He killed you."* I shook my head. *"How do I keep seeing you? Why are you not in Valhalla?"*

"Unfinished business." She smiled and nodded. *"I cannot let him destroy the world. No matter how small it is, I cannot let him ruin any more lives."*

I felt at a loss of words and just stood in astonishment as to how any of this was possible. *"How am I supposed to do that?"*

Her soft eyes met mine, and she smiled. *"Let your mother do the spell. You and your brother will be able to drive that dragon's blood sword through his heart. Together."*

I gasped. *"I don't have that sword anymore. I gave it to a friend."*

She nodded. *"I would suggest you get it back."*

"Does it have to be that sword?"

She shook her head. *"It just must be a strong one filled with magic, as no ordinary sword will work."*

I agreed silently, knowing that Izzy would not be happy. *"What are you not telling me?"*

She shook her head. *"There are some things that are better left unknown."* Her face became sad. *"Ragnar cursed me to this purgatory. It is peaceful here, but it is lonely. Once he is gone, I can be free. There is a consequence to using that sword against him. Dragon's blood is a very dangerous element to use. The sacrifice will end him, but it will not be without great loss."*

I stood, trying to absorb her words. *"Whomever uses the sword will die too, won't they?"*

She shrugged. *"All I can say is that immortality is not always as final as what you may think."*

And for the first time, the sound of immortality seemed to have a loophole. Maybe there was a way out of the spell after all. Maybe it would give me the strength I needed to drive the sword through his heart, then send me to Valhalla. I smiled and hoped that was the case. Only time would tell.

She smiled, and with that, the ghostly lady began to disappear and the cave came back into view. Izzy was standing over me with a bucket in hand as my brother and Mags were on both of my sides. I sat up, dripping wet and annoyed.

"What the hell?" I tried to wring out my shirt and let the water fall to the ground.

"You passed out!" Mags said frantically. "I tried to heal you, but you weren't waking up."

Izzy wiped her tears away. "I thought I killed you." She dropped to her knees and wrapped her arms around my neck, pulling my face into hers and kissing my lips frantically. "I'm so sorry," she whispered between kisses.

My brows furrowed in confusion. I grabbed her face and pulled her off me. "Iz, I'm fine." I laughed and stood up, pulling her up with me. "Geez, if you wanted to kiss me, you could've just asked. You didn't have to kill me first."

Her body trembled before she raised her hand and slapped my face before storming out of the cave.

My brother tsked me and nodded to follow her. Mags laughed quietly as if the moment was meant to be private.

Childish.

I rolled my eyes and knew today was not going to be a good day to ask for the sword back. I ran out of the cave to meet Izzy. I was still trying to wrap my head around the fact that her grandmother was coming to me in weird visions and wanting me to murder her father. How the hell was I supposed to tell her any of that? I needed to stay silent. Something inside me was begging me to bury the secret until it was needed.

"Iz, wait up."

She turned, and her glare stopped me in my tracks. "I thought I killed you," she screamed. "Do you have any idea what would happen to me if I killed the all high warrior and son of the Greystones? My father would rip my head off without thinking twice. Your death would be my death." She shoved me out of her space and huffed.

I exhaled slowly and grabbed her shoulders, pulling her back into me. "I don't know what happened, but it wasn't you. That I know for sure."

She shook her head.

"I know, it seems crazy, but I had some weird vision. I don't think it means anything, but it wasn't your fault."

Her brows furrowed. "A vision?" She crossed her arms. "I thought those were myths from the old stories… My father was rumored to destroy anyone with that sort of power."

"Let him come at me then." I shrugged. "Because it wasn't my first one."

Her jaw dropped. "And you're just telling me this now?"

I laughed. "Well, we've all been busy."

She swallowed hard and looked up at the night's sky. "What did you see?"

I shook my head. "Nothing that seems relevant right now." I turned around and hoped that would be good enough for her to drop it. "I'll tell you if I see anything else. Okay?"

She nodded. "I'm sorry I slapped you."

I laughed. "Just glad you didn't pull that right hook out on me."

She smirked. "Friends?" She held her hand out.

I nodded. "Friends."

# 9

Isadora Cambridge

I stared out of my bedroom window as the planets aligned above us. I had this sick feeling inside of me that something big was brewing and was going to tear my world apart, only I could not seem to figure out where it was stemming from. I watched as the otherworldly planets slowly moved, and something about the celestial event made me think that something big was coming. I inhaled slowly and watched them twinkle from afar, wondering what type of people were being held captive in those spheres. I wondered if maybe I'd be better off living there instead of here with my father.

"Hey, Izzy…" Mags walked up behind me, making me jump out of my own skin.

"Don't do that to me." I walked back to my bed and waited for her to join me. "What do you want?"

She inhaled slowly before I watched her eyes fill with tears ready to spill.

"Hey, hey, come here." I grabbed her and pulled her into me, trying to syphon her own struggles and let her rest her mind. "Don't cry, Mags, I'm here."

She sniffled and wiped her snot into the crook of my shoulder. "I heard Father talking to himself downstairs." She was trying to catch her breath. "Am I sick or something?"

I pulled her apart from me and examined her. "I mean, you don't seem sick… but he did say something like that the other day."

She fell back into my arms and bawled uncontrollably. "He said… he said… that you have to… syphon my magic out of me."

She rested her head on my lap and let me play with her hair, trying to soothe her the way our mother had done so many times before.

I shook my head. "Mags, Father thinks it will cure you." My brain began to seem fuzzy as the pit in my stomach grew larger, knowing that the words themselves didn't seem right to me, either.

Why wouldn't her healing magic heal her?

I shook my head. "That doesn't seem right, though, does it?"

She sat up and shook her head. "I don't want you to do it." She tucked her tear soaked hair behind her ear and reached for my hand. "Promise me you will not do it."

I stared back at her confused, feeling as though my brain and heart were battling inside me trying to emerge. "I can't let the sickness take you."

She squeezed my hand harder. "Izzy, I don't feel sick at all." Her doe eyes pleaded with me. "Promise me that you won't." She sniffled and swallowed hard. "I mean, what if by stealing my magic, you kill me?"

I huffed at her ridiculous thoughts and laughed softly. "I would never hurt you." I squeezed her hand back in reassurance. "You're my best friend. I would do anything to keep you safe. Even if I hate your obsession with all those boys."

She wiped her tears and laughed. "It's just Jimmy." She sniffled. "He's sweet to me."

I rolled my eyes. "There will be plenty of boys that will try and be sweet with you to join our lands together."

She shook her head. "Not like him." Her frown turned into a smile as she daydreamed. "I love him, Izzy."

"So gross." I shuddered and laughed as she joined me. "See, you don't need a silly boy to keep you safe. I can make you smile and protect you all the same." I pulled her back in for a hug and squeezed her tight. "I would never hurt you, Mags. I love you more than the moon, the stars, and those swirling planets up there. I would do anything to keep you safe."

She stared back at me and nodded. "I believe you." She smiled and kissed my cheek before standing and walking toward the doorway.

"Hey… I heard Mother whispering to Lady Greystone about 'taking care' of Father once and for all." Mags shrugged. "Honestly, I didn't want to know the details, but the sooner the better in my opinion."

I half smiled as the pit in my stomach grew and my head seemed to buzz. "I think you're right."

"I am." She smiled with confidence. "Goodnight."

"Goodnight."

I walked back over to the window and stared at the stupid planets, wondering how I could get a longship to sail away to one of them and leave this world far behind.

"My sweetest, Isadora. Come to me," my father's voice whispered, sending my body into a panic, a cold sweat spewing over me. Bile grew in the back of my throat. My body froze as my head began to buzz. I looked around the room for him but noticed I was alone in my own thoughts.

My body told me to run, but my brain began to move my feet toward the door and down the stairs. Mother was sleeping, and Mags had headed to her room already. I was truly alone and on my way to the man that I was torn between helping and running far far away from. I looked around our house and up and down the hallway, listening for his voice to send shivers through me again.

"Isadora," he whispered and then growled when my body accidentally slammed into him. I looked up, frightened, and waited for him to beat me for hurting him.

"I'm sorry," I said in an octave higher than I had intended. But my throat became as dry as a desert, and I no longer had any words left in me.

He looked down at me, and fear ran through me until his hardened face softened, and he smiled. "Oh, my beautiful daughter." His hand came up and grazed my cheek. "One more night, and the celestial event will be ready to harness from."

His smile became wide, and a spark shimmered in his eyes. For the first time in my life, the word "chaos" seemed relevant when it came not only to his lost magic, but also himself. I shuddered under his touch and nodded, trying to hold my fear from surfacing. The last thing I needed was for him to think that I was weak.

"I've concocted the henbane drink that your sister must take to start the syphoning."

I stayed silent and frozen in place.

"The last ingredient needed is a teensy tiny drop of your blood." he shrugged, innocently. "Just a little prick, and it will be ready."

I fidgeted with my hands and stared at my fingertips.

"Yes, right there, sweetheart."

"Father, I don't think this is a good idea." I shook my head, finally finding my voice. "Mother and Mags think that I should stay away from you."

He growled. "Wasteful witches. They will be the first to go."

I leaned back, wanting to get as far away from him for tonight.

"Syphon," he cleared his throat, "I mean, Isadora, my child. Please." He held his hand out and waited.

I shook my head. "No, Father. This is wrong."

"Give me your hand, and your blood will help heal the world."

I felt the buzz in my head as the pit in my stomach grew. "Okay." I lifted my hand and reached out toward him.

He grabbed my wrist and pricked my finger, catching the crimson red into a small jar and staring at it in amusement. "Now, get some sleep. Tomorrow will be here before we know it." He smiled. "Here, take this with you, and make sure she drinks it."

I nodded and headed back toward my room with the small vile enclosed in my palm. A sickness grew inside me as my world felt as if it would begin to crumble.

I obeyed and laid down in my bed, praying to the gods for a restful night and a clear head in the morning.

The morning light blinded me as I groaned to roll out of bed. I could hear my sister's door open before the footsteps reached my door. Whispers beyond my hearing grew louder before my door creaked open.

"Come on, little love. Time to go for a walk," my mother's voice whispered. She held Mags hand to follow. She slowly closed my door and came next to me on the bed.

I rubbed my eyes, trying to process what was happening.

"Now, come on. A little lady time with my favorite girls."

"We're your only girls," Mags groaned from behind her sleepily.

She softly laughed. "Of course you are. Now come. Get dressed."

I obeyed and stood, reaching for my clothes and quickly dressing, placing the vile in my pocket secretly as she opened the door and looked down the hallway. She nodded, and within a minute, we were on our way to the open field. I smiled as the three of us walked hand in hand across the land with the sun beaming down on us. I felt whole again. They were my happiness, and I prayed it stayed that way for once.

Chapter 10
Eric Greystone

I couldn't sleep. Instead, I spent the whole night awake with my sword in hand, watching Izzy's house from a distance. My brother fell asleep halfway through the night, but I knew he needed sleep more than either of us, so I let him be. On the battlefield, I had gone multiple nights on very little sleep. I knew that I could fully function on very little. The sun began to rise along the bluffs, and in a moment's notice, I watched stirring in the Cambridge home. My eyes followed Lady Cambridge as she walked to Mag's room and then headed to Izzy's. I looked down at Ragnar's chambers and watched as his room stayed still.

What are they doing?

I squinted and watched as they snuck around the home before heading in my direction. I quickly ran over by Jimmy and dragged him into the bush with me, shushing him into silence. He stared back at my wide eyes as he began to orient himself.

"Shhhh." He looked past me and saw the Cambridge's headed in our direction.

"Shit." He pulled me down further and buried us into the bushes.

As the ladies passed, we both finally exhaled and burst into laughter.

"That was close," Jimmy said. "Too close."

I laughed again and nodded. "Come on, let's follow them."

Jimmy grabbed my arm as I tried to stand. "Maybe we shouldn't… What if they are having a private moment?"

I huffed. "Brother, Izzy is on a mission to kill her sister. We need to keep an eye on her. Her father has a hold on her, and we can't let anything happen to her."

He thought about it for a minute and nodded. "Fine, but keep a distance, just in case."

I nodded, and we ran quietly behind them, staying out of sight.

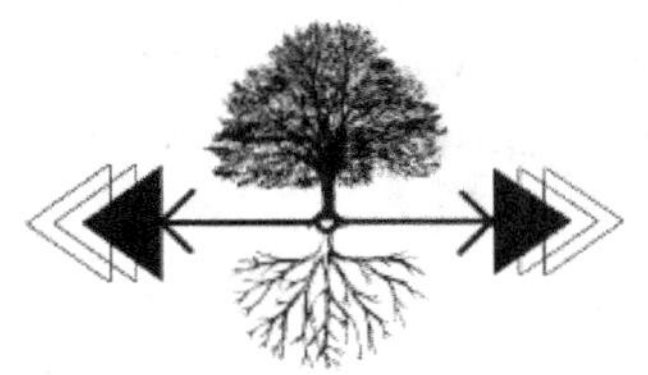

They walked into the cave—our cave. I listened as their voices began to fade. "Okay, let's get closer." We creeped slowly in and listened.

"Girls, a lot has happened, and I know you are too young to understand any of this."

Izzy huffed in annoyance.

"No, even you, Isadora. You are both too young for any of this, and I am sorry to have involved you, but I am not sorry to be your mother." I heard Lady Cambridge sniffle. "You two have been the best thing about my entire life, and I would not change a thing."

"Mother, what is happening?" Mags asked.

I reached the last boulder that would give us coverage and slowed, peeking past it and watching them interact.

"I need you girls to do exactly as I say." Lady Cambridge inhaled heavily. Her chest was shaking with sadness. "I need both of you to stay here while I take care of some things back home. Promise me that you will not come home until I give you the all clear."

Izzy sneered. "What is going on?"

Her mother grabbed her shoulders and sternly kept her attention. "You must stay away from your father tonight. He has plans with the celestial alignment, and if you are anywhere near him, then he will use you and try to get into your mind."

Izzy shook her head in disbelief as Mags stared wide eyed at the severity of the situation they were in.

We watched as Lady Cambridge lifted her dress slightly, exposing her thigh, which made both my brother and I quickly look away before a shimmering dagger attached to her thigh in a sheath came into her possession. It was hidden perfectly under her dress. I stared at the Obsidian blade with a handle that seemed to be made out of an animal's jaw. I looked at the sharp teeth at the end and listened carefully.

"This is a Hildisvini dagger. A pagan family, the Meadows, a few lands over created it years ago. Do you remember Aislynn Meadows?" The girls nodded. "Her mother was able to create this prison world inside of here. Your father used to use this blade to kill witches to strengthen his chaos magic. He will never suspect that we have altered it. We can trap your father in until the Greystone boys are able to do their immortality spell to kill him. And even that is a small chance at success against him. Their mother is not ready for the spell and we are running out of time. We must take action now."

Izzy and Mags both gasped as she held out the dagger for them to examine.

"Aislynn's mother made this?" Izzy questioned and grabbed the blade.

"She has some of the oldest spells in her grimoires passed down through generations beyond our existence."

I looked back at my brother, wide eyed, as we had never heard of the Meadows family. We both shrugged and kept listening.

"Neither of you will be able to get him out of it. He will be permanently trapped until he can be destroyed. Nothing can get out until it has been unlocked by your bloodline or a syphon. Neither of you can do it. When you are much older and have heirs of your own, one drop of your child's blood will be able to release anyone from the dagger. Do you understand?"

Izzy and Mags looked at each other and then back to their mother.

"Why would we ever release anyone from it?" Mags asked. "If he's locked away, then we will keep him that way."

Her mother nodded. "We will need to tell Eric and Jimmy about the dagger and we will help them transport into the dagger one day when they are strong enough to destroy him. Do you understand? Their mother is not ready for this and I truly can't blame her. So, unfortunately, we've had to change plans. Your father is becoming stronger each day, and we are out of time. I can't have him destroying anymore families for power."

Izzy stood silently. "Where will you be?"

Lady Cambridge inhaled slowly. "I will be back. I need to talk to Lady Greystone and tell her our change of plans so she can sleep better tonight until her husband is home. And I also need to do one more thing. To keep you safe."

They nodded silently.

I watched as her mother looked down at the string of leather around her neck and then back at the wall and grunted. She checked her pockets once more. "I forgot the hagstone." She inhaled slowly and shook her head. "Here, put this on and stay here. I will have to go and get it from the house to show you the rest."

"The rest of what?" Mags asked.

She handed Izzy the leather but seemed in deep thought. Izzy went to place it over her head but jolted it back.

"Ew, that smells like death."

"You need to wear that. I'll bring the hagstone back, and it'll make you forget about the smell." Her mother shushed her lips. "I don't know when he's listening." She shook her head. "You two spend the rest of the day here, and I will come for you after the planets pass one another. Do not come home whatever you do. Stay here. I will bring the hagstone back."

They nodded, obeying their mother's orders.

"Mags, where is your Labradorite necklace?"

Mags looked down to her chest and panicked.

"I must've left it on my nightstand."

Her mother frowned. "I will bring it back with me. I won't be long."

Mags smiled and nodded.

Their mother smiled and kissed them both. "Here is everything you will need for the day. Food, water, supplies." She pulled them both in for a hug. "Just stay put my little loves." Izzy wrapped her arm around Mags and held her as their mother let go of their embrace.

I quickly tapped Jimmy and nodded toward the exit. We needed to disappear and fast. We took off and ran for the open field.

When we put enough distance between us and them, we finally dropped to the ground and tried to catch our breath.

"What do… you think we… should do?" my brother asked worriedly.

I shrugged, trying to wrap my own head around the panic already caused by the stupid planets aligning. The sun had only rose minutes ago and we couldn't even see the damn things floating in the sky yet.

I yelled and threw my shield across the field. I grabbed the earth with my palms and let magic flow through my veins and rip apart the field. "Damn it. Damn it all. I didn't want any of this."

Jimmy reached me and tried to pull me back to reality, but reality sucked.

"Let go of me," I yelled and pushed him off. I could feel my chest race as I tried to control my anger. But I hated every bit about this. I hated the magic I was born with and the strength that I could hold, only to be weak in a moment of doing what's right for my own selfish being of not wanting to have immortality or need to kill my friend's father. No matter how evil he was, he was still her blood.

I dropped to my knees and fiercely pierced the ground with my fists and let my magic flow through me sending waves of magic through parts of the field that seemed to rumble the earth. I looked up, breathing heavily as the lone small tree shook back and forth before it spiraled up and grew to a full grown tree, fully bloomed and no longer a pathetic little tree that would surely die during winter this year. Instead it became a magnificent wonder in the middle of the open field with deep roots.

I smirked as I stood and wiped the dirt off me, heading toward it. My brother ran to catch up with me and met me under the branches.

"Holy shit." Jimmy stood in amazement and laid his hand on the tree trunk. "Talk about a magical object right in front of us." He looked back at me. "How did you do that?"

I caught my breath and shrugged. "I don't know."

He stared back at me and examined my palms, which were still glowing from the exertion.

"Remember when you used to bring me to that other world? The middle," he asked. I looked up and nodded. "Do you think it stems from black magic like Ragnar can do?"

I huffed. "Neither that place nor this is dark magic. And I am nothing like Ragnar. Do you see how beautiful this tree is? And has the middle ever felt evil to you? They do not come from dark magic… I would never tap into that."

He eyed me and shrugged. "I'm just saying, I've never seen magic like yours." He swallowed and shook his head. "I mean… I can do some things, but I've never been able to tap into other dimensions nor grow a tree."

I shrugged. "We're all a little different… I guess."

He nodded and crossed his arms. "Guess so. Seems like you got the better deal."

"Guess so." We laughed as I grasped my palms and tried to soothe the feeling of ice growing over them.

We both stared at the wonder now in front of us for a minute longer. "We need to go check on the twins."

He nodded, and we ran back to the cave.

"What are you guys doing here?" I slowed my pace once I saw the two of them sitting on the boulder in the center of the cave.

Izzy jumped when she heard my voice and turned quickly with her palms ablaze. I smirked at her. She dropped her hands and came running into my arms, hugging me tight as if I were her last lifeline on earth that could save her. I raised my eyebrows at Mags and wondered what else I had missed.

"Our mother is going to trap our father tonight." She wiped her eyes.

I swallowed hard and lifted Izzy, carrying her back to the boulder to set her down gently and rub her shoulders.

"I thought this is what we wanted?"

Mags shrugged slowly and sniffled. "He's not a good man, but he's still our father."

"What can we do to help?" I asked, but neither of them seemed to know the answer.

An hour passed with no sign of their mother's return. Both Jimmy and I glanced back to one another, and both had the same idea. Something wasn't right. A shift in the world was happening. and with Lady Cambridge not back yet, we both knew that whatever her plan was, it was no longer going as planned.

Mags and Izzy began to look back and forth with worry. I knew they could feel it too.

Jimmy sat down quietly next to Mags and held her hand.

"Why don't we run away from all of this? You and I start a life somewhere off these lands and have a fresh start?" He looked back at me, and I nodded in agreement.

She looked up to him and without hesitation, she nodded. "Okay." She looked back to Izzy, who seemed to silently know it was the right decision.

"Eric, you look after Izzy and meet us across the river when everything is done tonight."

I nodded. "Just get out of here, and get as far away from these lands as you can. Something's not right."

Mags jumped up and hugged her sister tight. "I will see you soon?"

Izzy nodded and half smiled before seeming to be in her own world of thoughts.

"Hey, you okay?"

She looked back at me and seemed so confused. "Can you hear that too?"

I stared back at her confused and shook my head. "Hear what?"

She swallowed hard and stood. "I need my sword. It's back at home. If we're running, then I need it."

I grabbed mine from the sheath behind me and handed it to her. "Take mine."

She shook her head. "No, I need the dragon's blood one. I need something with magic to syphon from if I ever plan on killing him." She began to walk toward the entrance as Mags and my brother followed.

I huffed. "You're not going to be the one to kill him…" She froze and turned back around, letting the others keep moving. "I am."

She walked back toward me and sneered, "Why you?"

I felt a pain in my heart as I realized the hurt I would cause her in the long run. I shook my head, knowing that I had already said too much.

"Iz, just stay here. I will go and get your sword and make sure that Mags and my brother get far enough away."

She seemed so torn between herself and whatever was in her head that I felt sorry for her.

"Just wait here, please, Iz… for me."

She bit her bottom lip and looked down at the ground. She sniffled and then nodded without looking back up.

I hugged her tight and turned to meet up with the others. "I'll be back for you, I promise."

My brother had stopped running and was carrying Mags over his shoulder, marching back toward me.

"Woah, what's going on?"

He huffed as Mags demanded to be let down. "She's trying to go back home to grab a few things."

I laughed while still trying to catch my breath. "Are you out of your damn mind, Mags? Your mother wants you nowhere near that place."

She kicked Jimmy straight in the stomach, making him drop to his knees and set her down. Grabbing his abdomen, he groaned in pain.

"Yeah, well, I forgot my mother's necklace at home on my nightstand. I can't leave town without it. It's one of the things my mother went back for."

I rolled my eyes.

"I can't leave without it. You don't understand."

"Stupid girls and their sentimental possessions." I sighed heavily, trying to reroute my own plan. "Listen, I'll go and grab it. I have to get Izzy's sword too. Just don't go any closer to your home please." I looked down at my brother and laughed. "And see… that's exactly why I don't need you in my way against their father."

He laughed and winced when he touched his lower rib. "Broken rib isn't going to get me far at all at this point."

I looked down and saw the protruding bone under his skin. "Damn, Mags. Can you heal him?"

She looked down in shock. "I'm so sorry. I didn't mean to. Here, let me help you." She dropped to her knees and placed her palms over his torso. "Stop squirming," she demanded and rolled her eyes.

"Well, it hurts."

She smirked. "Serves you right, laying your hands on a lady like that."

I laughed and nodded. "She's right, big brother. You need to learn some manners in the presence of a lady."

Magic began to flow from her healing hands onto his broken rib. He winced once more before biting his lower lip and closing his eyes before we heard the bone snap back into place.

He jumped up and examined his torso, looking down in amusement and smiling.

"Just stay here with her. I'll be back soon with the sword and necklace." They both nodded as I ran for the bluffs to climb down.

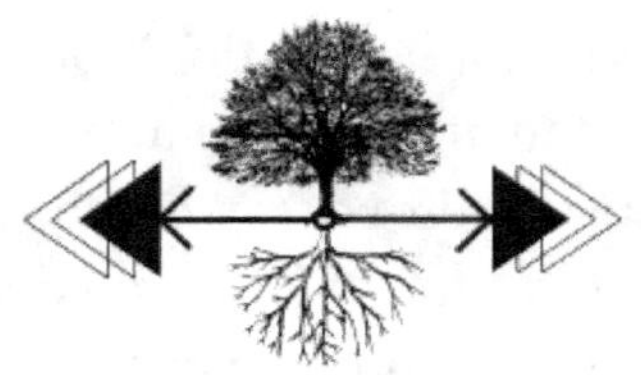

The house seemed to have a shiver to it. It was still summer, but the chill of winter surrounded their house above. I crept closer and scouted the home, only it seemed as if the place was abandoned. Then, I saw movement and lowered myself to the hill before deciding on my best entry and exit points.

Only Oxana was standing there with her hands in the air and scaly wings spreading wider underneath her. My entire body froze as I watched her fingernails grow and curl into claws, and her face became distorted into a fire breathing dragon as her whole body shapeshifted in front of my eyes. The roof began to shake as she was outgrowing the small confinement. She glared down at Ragnar standing in front of steam coursing from her nostrils, and a low growl began to grow from her scaly chest.

My eyes widened as everything happened so fast—the roof began to break, and I watched helplessly as both my mother and father came running to Oxana's and Lady Cambridge's aid. My mother ran with her meticulous magic charging in her palms, and my father created a

92

tornado of wind and debris to tear apart the house further.

"We're too late!" my mother yelled, as they charged the house. "He's found his chaos magic."

I tried to run after them and join them in the fight, but for the first time in my life, I could not move. I felt like a coward as the dragon grew and my parents began to attack Ragnar. Lady Cambridge was thrown back against the wall as Ragnar began to beat her with unrecognizable strength. My parents tried everything they could to release her and get between them. Lady Cambridge's head hit the wall hard one last time before her body crumbled underneath her and she fell to the floor, unconscious. I tried to stand to help her, but my body lowered into the ground further. I could feel tears rolling down my cheeks as my mind screamed at me to help them.

Help them all.

"Damn it." I pushed myself off the ground and pulled my sword from its sheath, glad that I had kept it with me, and ran for the house, my legs feeling like jelly. I needed to be strong at this very moment. I pushed past the gate, and it was the biggest mistake of my life.

My mother turned around and stared at me in shock, losing contact for one brief second as Ragnar turned, smirking and lifting the dagger off the ground. In one swift motion, he beheaded both my parents.

I felt as if I had been kicked in the chest as my entire world collapsed, their bodies fell to the ground as Oxana's dragon began to churn fire down onto Ragnar, extinguishing not only him but my parent's lifeless bodies, and everything inside me altered.

Rage.

Anger.

Hatred.

Kill him... Kill him... Kill him...

I grabbed my sword and ran for him, slicing my blade through the air and aiming for his head. I could feel every emotion inside of me explode as my own magic gripped the sword, and my hands glowed with red and black twirling around my grip—too much power, too much darkness trying to take over me. I yelled as I let the magic decide and sliced Ragnar's face nearly in half. He was pushed back by Oxana's clawed foot that was ready to come crashing down on him, my blade slicing his face, leaving a wicked scar for him to have while he's waiting at the gates of Hell.

Then, my world stopped. I felt the wet liquid begin to drip down my chest as the sting of the blade pierced my chest, Ragnar on the other end of it. He smirked as he turned the dagger into me like a clock dial and pushed me to the ground, pulling the dripping dagger from me.

My chest rose, and my lungs felt as if they were collapsing. My surroundings began to spin as I no longer felt as though I could grasp the earth's ground anymore.

Death.

My death?

How?

My eyes became heavy as the world disappeared.

Isadora Cambridge

He was taking too long. I couldn't wait here any longer. I huffed and jumped off the boulder and walked toward the entrance of the cave. I let the warm sun reach my face and closed my eyes, soaking in the sun's powers of happiness. I looked around, and in all the silence, I felt truly alone. I hated being separated from Mags.

And what if she was really going to run off with the Greystone brother?

Stupid.

I grabbed the pungent piece of leather and ripped it from my neck, irritated that Mags had Mother's beautiful stone and I got the ugly piece of leather that smelled like manure. I just wanted to be back with Mags so I could keep her safe and heal her from her sickness.

But then my father's voice haunted me, and something about him wanting me to *heal* her didn't seem right either.

I knelt down and placed my palms over the earth, letting my magic pull from the core. Only, as I began to syphon slowly, a pull toward home began to make me feel sick. Something was wrong—I could feel it. My forearm began to tingle and then glowed as an image of Eric appeared as if he was standing in front of me. But something was wrong with him. He was bleeding and alone.

"No," I yelled, as I lifted my skirt and bunched it into my fists to run toward the direction I was to stay far away from.

I slowed, trying to catch my breath, and began to panic as I saw smoke rising from our lands. I furrowed my brows and tried to get a closer look, only for the pit in my stomach to grow.

"Damn it." I inhaled heavily and let my feet carry me faster.

I came to a complete halt when I saw what was supposed to be my home, but a black dragon with fire orange scales shimmering along its body was taking up the entire space. I watched cautiously as I tried to plan my best attack on the dragon to save my lands from becoming a complete graveyard. The people of our hometown began panicking, and instead of fighting with magic, they were running away from the danger.

"Hey, stop!" I tried to grab the arm of a few of the townspeople, pleading for their help. "Cowards," I yelled, as they escaped and ran for the trees. I shook my head and scouted the best entrance of surprise to attack the beautiful, yet dangerous creature. I had never seen one alive, only stories from centuries ago of them flying freely and co-existing with us on our lands. Stories of when they could be flown and rode along with them into battle or just enough to be free from the lands and explore the world that we only were existing in.

Then, a piercing scream coursed through my veins as I recognized Mags and Jimmy standing over a boy, Mags frantically using her power to try and heal him. I tried to adjust my eyes and see who was on the ground, then panicked as I saw Eric's face. My feet ran faster than I had ever done before. I crashed into Jimmy and knelt down next to Eric, lifting his arm and grabbing his hand and interlocking his fingers with mine, praying to the old gods and new ones that they let him live.

The dragon seemed to look right at us and almost blocked us from the danger that was looming underneath it. I looked around its tail and saw my father swinging his sword into the air, charging his other palm with a green power that I had never seen him use before.

I stood, confused, and watched in a daze trying to place how the hell he got his magic back. Then, I saw it…

The glowing Jasper stone was glowing from a hemp necklace along his chest.

"Bastard," I growled. *He figured it out. I activated it, and now he was able to use it on his own.* "Damn it."

I looked at him and the dragon and couldn't decide who I was supposed to help. A part of me said to syphon the creature's supernatural ability away while another told me my father was causing chaos in our town.

"Izzy, you need to help your mother," Jimmy yelled and grabbed my arm, pulling me back to reality. His eyes welled with tears as he pointed toward my mother laying on the ground unconscious and then I saw the others. I gasped and recognized what was left of Lady Greystone's armor that she always wore across her wrists.

"No, no, no… I can fix this… I can—"

"Just help yours before you end up alone."

I nodded and ran toward my mother, trying to wake her as my father and the dragon went back and forth. Suddenly the rumbling ground calmed and the shadow of the dragon disappeared, letting the quickly setting sun blind me as I tried to wake my mother. I looked toward the sky and saw nothing flying away.

My father smirked as he twisted Oxana's amulet in the air in a circular motion and tsked his tongue. "Weak dragon."

I let the shock factor settle as I watched the amulet's glow disappear and realized whatever he had done had trapped that poor dragon in another world. I turned back to my mother and shook her violently, realizing that the dragon had been on our side after all and now it was me against the man that terrified me. "Please, Mother, please wake up."

She stirred underneath me, and shock crossed her face.

"No, you shouldn't be here. Leave now. Leave!" she screamed and pushed me away from her. "Where's your necklace?" She tried to refocus her eyes and rubbed her head as her eyes widened. I looked down and realized I ruined part of her plan. If only she would've told me more and not looked at me like such a child… I could handle it. "Go, now."

I stumbled back and fell to the earth, trying to figure out what was going on.

It was my father's voice that made me nauseous as he reached his hand out to me to pull me back on my feet. "Come, child, it's time."

I shook my head. "The dragon? Where did… The Greystones… Eric… Mother?" I inhaled heavily. "What is happening?" I rejected his help and jumped to my feet. Palms ablaze, trying to rummage through my head and place the puzzle pieces in order. I looked up at the sky and saw the planet's inch in line as the moon began to rise, and the bright spheres glowed ominously and aligned perfectly. Only, instead of the world imploding, it became clear what had happened.

I turned on my father and began to fight him off. I charged my palms and let the fire rise as I released it in his direction and made his fresh cut sizzle as it scarred his face. The wound no longer dripped but crusted over with burned blood. He smirked, and I knew I was not going to win this one.

He walked slowly over to me, charging his palms with a green and black magic swirling around them. I watched as his chaos magic seemed to flow unevenly in a distorted way that seemed unnatural compared to our magic.

Fear grew inside me.

I threw another fireball at him, hitting him in the face again, only he didn't even seemed phased by it and continued to walk until he was directly in front of me. He lifted me into the air by my throat, choking me as the black stands of chaos surrounded my neck and began to crawl down my entire body, I felt my skin creeping as it crawled around me and then through me. His darkness found every opening it could, and I felt like my soul left my body. I watched from above as his magic coursed into me and circled my brain. I could feel the burning inside my head as I watched before I was pulled back into my body, only to have my entire body feel as if it had been burned alive. I was boiling from the inside out, and I needed to run. I needed to get as far away as possible. I needed to get out of this body that was burning to death. Or I just needed to die.

I needed to die.

I grasped my palms around his wrist and began to syphon as much as I could, in hopes of weakening him for a brief second, but instead, I felt the poison swimming faster inside of me. I screamed in pain as the realization settled, knowing that this would be how I would die—at the hands of my father.

My father's grip loosened as Jimmy took his sword and pierced it into his back, making him drop to his knees for the briefest moment, giving me relief from the torture and letting my lungs expand. I jumped up and wrapped both my hands around my father's throat, tightening them so no oxygen could enter.

"You will never hurt me again," I screamed, as I let rage take over. I took the Jasper stone and ripped it from his neck. It had to be what was helping his power grow. And unfortunately, if this wasn't his full potential, then I would hate to see how much more strength he would have with any more magic. I spat at him and began to crush his throat.

My father looked up at me and smirked as Jimmy's hands raised the sword into the air. I looked at my father in disgust and nodded to Jimmy in approval. I released my hands and waited for him to end this. End all of this. For me, for Mags, for his parents, for Eric, for our homelands. But he froze and then brought the sword down with wide eyes for help.

"Iz, help—"

I gasped as he forced his sword into his own abdomen and dropped to the ground, bleeding out rapidly as his body trembled.

"No," I screamed. "Mags help!" I turned and watched as Mags jumped off Eric and ran to his brother. She quickly placed her healing palms along his wound and applied pressure. Everything happened so fast that before I could even react, my body froze in place and the burning sensation came back to me, making my entire body tremble.

"Now, sweet Syphon of mine. The planets are ready, and there is no one left to help you escape. It's time to finish what we started. One last sacrifice to make me indestructible."

I shook my head, trying to shake my father's voice from rambling inside me.

"Get away from me."

Mags looked up to me confused.

"Not you. Heal him faster," I pleaded with her.

She nodded and began to whisper incantations, which seemed to seal the wound much faster.

"Take my blade, and pierce it through your sister's heart."

I shook my head and choked on my own scattered thoughts.

I looked at Mags and shook my head, then went back to my father, who nodded. "Yes, child. Now."

"I can't." My body was frozen in place, but every emotion began to flow through me as I no longer felt in control of my own body or mind.

"Isadora?" My mother's voice called from behind me, as she struggled to her feet and tried to limp toward me. Mags ran to her and healed her leg as fast as she could before our mother threw her labradorite necklace across Mags neck and pushed her away. "Run, my sweetheart," she said to Mags, kissing her forehead. "Isadora, take her and run. Now!"

I watched my mother and let the tears fall in defeat.

"I can't move." I panicked and tried to loosen his mind from me. "Mother, he's got me."

"Damn it." She began to run toward Ragnar. Charging her magic and letting the pink hummingbirds multiply, she raised her palms and released them in the air at him, throwing him at a distance that may have been far enough away for a minute to let us escape. I felt my legs unlock as his mind control unlinked itself, and I was able to breathe for a second.

Jimmy was healed, and Eric's chest was rising again. Everything seemed to be okay for the slightest moment.

"Oh, Mags," I cried, as I dropped to the ground and wrapped my arms around her, squeezing her tightly and embracing the only lifeline I had holding me together. "We need to leave. We need to get far away. They will be okay now."

102

She cried as she hugged me tighter and nodded. "We will come back for them?"

I nodded, knowing we could never come back. We stood up and began to run away from our broken home. I looked up to my bedroom window that was only partially left and climbed the side of the wall. "Hold on, I need my sword." I scaled the wall and climbed through the window. Shaking my head at the damage that could never be repaired here, I went under my bed and grabbed the sword before climbing back down.

I grabbed Mags's hand, and we began to run until my body froze and the sickness consumed me again.

"No running. Get back here."

"Mags, I need you to run. Father is trying to control me."

She shook her head and squeezed my hand tighter. "I'm not leaving you."

"Just go! I will find you," I yelled.

"I'm not leaving you," she cried. "I love you, Izzy. I can't just leave you."

My head burned as my thoughts were no longer mine. I turned around and watched as our father was getting closer to us, and every thought I tried to have as my own disappeared. All I could think about was curing Mags and taking her magic.

It's the only way.

"Drink this." I grabbed the vile and forced it down her throat.

"Heal her…syphon her magic…It's the only way… Don't let her magic go to waste… Syphon it out as you pierce her heart."

I saw our mother trying to reach us but was being pulled back by Ragnar every chance he could get. It was an impossible grasp to get past. I looked back at Mags with tear filled eyes as she tried to release my grasp and began to scream as my syphoning began to flow. I saw my hand reach for the dagger on the ground before my entire world became black, and I prayed that death would meet me before anything bad happened to Mags.

I stood shaking as my surroundings reappeared. I looked down and dropped the bloodied dagger from my grasp, letting it vibrate the world as it hit the ground, sending a flash of anger throughout the lands.

"What did *you* do, what did *I* do, what did *you* make me do?" I grabbed my sister in my arms as her lifeless body became heavier in my hands. "No… Mags? Please, Mags, wake up. Mags, please." My entire body shook, and my magic didn't feel stronger—in fact, I felt that something was missing from me. I tried to syphon from the earth to try and heal her, then gasped as I realized my syphoning was gone entirely. I looked to my palms and tried to syphon from the ground again, to pull any kind of element that would bring my sister back. "What did *you* make me do?" I screamed at my father, who had just finished hitting my mother for the last time as she groaned on the ground, failing to get back up.

"Whiny child, why do you care so much? She was weak."

"She's my sister, I love her," I yelled and tried to wipe the tears that wouldn't stop falling.

He scoffed. "You want power, and with her in your way, you will get nothing."

I sobbed uncontrollably as I tried to wake Mags. "I don't want power. I want her alive."

"Oh, Syphon, I didn't want to do this, but you just don't stop, do you? Just like your mother with that pathetic heart." He knelt down beside me and pushed Mags body out of my arms before grabbing my shoulders. "Turn it off."

"Let go of me." I thrashed in his arms and tried to release his grip.

"I said, turn. It. Off."

"No." I spat in his face and tried to knock his head with mine, only to be pinned to the ground. His eyes locked with mine as his hands steadied my head from moving.

"Turn them off," he screamed.

I tried to plug my ears, but his hands swatted them away. I tried to close my eyes and imagine the cave or the field or anywhere that would let me get quiet and peace or at least as much space I needed to get away from this psychopath. Space from Mags's dead body, space for my head to clear, space from the world I just destroyed.

My world.

My happiness.

My sister.

I kicked him in the groin, and he released me just long enough for me to try and head for the field.

I froze when his voice came back into my head. Before I knew it, I was thrown back into the wall of the last remaining brick to our broken home. I could hear the fragile bones inside me snap. I watched painfully as he charged back toward me and locked me in his death grip. "Turn off your feelings, Syphon. Power and my allegiance are what you crave. Your sister was weak," he spat. "You are strong." He began to choke me until I felt my head become light again and the world stopped spinning. "Turn off that switch that cares so much… Now!" I could feel him trying to persuade my own thoughts as I tried to fight him off both physically and mentally, but my brain began to feel scrambled in my head. My ears began to buzz with a ringing so deafening that made me think that I would be better off to die. And then… there it was. The last shield I had trying to protect myself and my family was broken. I felt my entire body shift as my brain began to re-route itself as he stripped the last human bone I had left in me.

"Power," I whispered, as he slowly released his grip. "I want power." I nodded, and I knew exactly what my purpose was in life.

I needed this.

I needed more.

Power.

I watched as my mother, bruised and bloodied, came running toward us, screaming to let me go. She came charging and lifted the Hildisvian blade from where I had dropped it, and it came slashing above my head, straight for my father's face. I watched as the tip slit his recent wound from his eye to his chin back open, and blood gushed from the site, finally forcing him to release me as he fell to the ground. I gasped for air to refill my empty lungs. My head pounded as the word *power* haunted me, but my own being believed it was exactly the right course I was on. I needed to protect him and myself from anyone that tried to take him away from me. He wanted what *I* wanted, and together *we'd* conquer this pathetic world and have all the power to ourselves.

Seconds passed as I looked up and watched the two of them forcefully slamming each other from side to side on our lands that we had fought so hard to keep, magic coursing through their veins as they thrashed one another. I smirked at my mother's weakness compared to him and attempted to stand and try to save him from her wrath because he was here to help *me*, help *us,* become powerful and that's what I *wanted.*

I raised my palms and yelled, "Ignis," and forced them apart with flames. Everything seemed to happen in slow motion as I walked to her and grabbed her wrist, trying to syphon from her, but nothing happened again. Instead, I felt my head start to become lighter and more clear.

Wait... What am I doing?

My stomach became queasy as I realized what my *father* was doing to *me*. He was messing with my mind, making me become someone I was not and never would be. He was making me into his little puppet. I looked up at my mother in horror for anything that I had unintentionally done as tears started to flow. My very own chaos was surrounding me as the flash of goodness tried to pull its way back into me.

"Help me, Mother," I begged.

My body could feel the tugging of inner peace and happiness from my mother and the sickness and dark from my father, both twirling around inside of me and as I battled with my own mind and kept them both separated across from me. I watched as black and green swirls with pink swirls began to circle me before growing large around me and engulfing me as their own magic closed in.

I looked to my mother with fear and watched as she looked over to Mags laying on the floor and shook her head in sadness before flicking her palm open, releasing a pink hummingbird toward me. As it charged me, she mouthed, "I'm sorry, my little love." The tiny bird came at me and exploded against the pink and green fighting to take over me, and everything disappeared, along with the hold I had on my parents to keep them apart.

My mother stood and took the Hildisvan dagger, pushing past me as she stabbed my father's heart with it and in an instant, my mind felt like a slingshot. Every good vision I was beginning to see clearly disappeared, and rage filled my head again as she and him disappeared into thin air. I stood alone with a broken home and without a single family member left to love me. I picked up my blade and looked one last time at Mags before running for the trees and never looking back at the chaos that once was here.

10 years later...

Isadora Cambridge

I watched as the night's sky mimicked the planets shifting a decade ago. The full moon glowed brighter than usual, and I followed the glow to my forearm that now left a Mark of two triangles interlocking. I hated the damn thing. It appeared a few years ago while I was out in the woods, trying to find shelter for the night's storm brewing. It was the only light that I had to find an abandoned cave, which was still close enough to the new town that I had decided to make my own home, where no one knew me. I needed a fresh start. A new beginning away from the orphan who killed her own sister.

I wiped my tears as I knew I would have to wait out the storm in here before getting lost in the woods again. I looked around the cave and lifted my palms to the ceiling and let my magic flow through me, clearing the boulder above and opening the sky, letting the lightning flicker as the rain spattered down onto the covering above like a glass shield protecting me. I grabbed my satchel and laid it under my head as I watched the dark stormy sky ignite as something inside of me started to crawl.

"Find him, Syphon. Find the dagger and release me."

I shook my head and plugged my ears. "Leave me alone."

"Release me, child."

"Get out of my head," I screamed and threw a fireball toward the cave entrance that was empty. My father's voice continued to haunt me—ten years as I tried to restart my life, and I still had the sickness of darkness inside me. But instead of giving into it, I battled daily trying to keep the dark magic from consuming my soul. If I could at least save my soul, then I may have a chance at redemption in Valhalla. I prayed to the old gods and the new ones, that they could forgive me for the sickness taking over me. Forgive me for my father's mind tricks controlling my actions.

"I would never hurt my sister… I never meant to," I whispered, as my ears began to burn from squeezing them too tight to keep his voice from echoing inside me.

I let the tears flow as I closed my eyes and tried to get some sleep despite the storm that was brewing outside of me. Whether that was the real storm or the one with *his* voice trying to control me, I hadn't decided yet.

I unplugged my ears and let my forearm gently glow the closer I came back to my old lands. I knew I could never set foot there again, but I always felt a pull toward the place since the last solar eclipse occurred. I remembered that was the night that I seemed to always be drawn toward my old lands again.

The glow continued and seemed to have a mind of its own as the ominous light put me to sleep, and for once, my head was silent as I let my body and head rest peacefully.

The morning came early, but I felt rested. I yawned and stretched out my arms, trying to see the mirage opened ceiling as the clouds zoomed past me. I smiled and decided to head to the market for trades today. I grabbed my satchel and opened it to make sure the honey from Lenora, the beekeeper that had been letting me stay with her for the last few years, was undamaged and still sellable. I took one jar out after counting them and opened the lid, dipping my finger inside and taking a swoop out of it for breakfast.

I let the honey drip off my fingertip and onto my tongue, the sweet sensation sending a jittering through my body with its sweetness. "That damn witch cheated again." I took another dip into the honey and smiled as I ate it. "Magic infused honey, a drug to anyone to keep them coming back for more." I laughed as I sealed the jar back up and placed it carefully into my satchel. *Lenora.* I smiled and rolled my eyes as I put it across my shoulder and headed for the sunlight.

The market was packed today. The towns from many lands seemed to gather as they made their way slowly up and down each table to trade their works for another more grand. I held my satchel close to protect the jars as I inched my way toward the table that was promised to be open for me to place the honey for sale for Lenora.

"Excuse me," I said, as I grazed passed each person. My forearm began to tingle and then itch the closer I got to it. I stopped walking and examined it. My Mark was not glowing but almost seemed to have a pulse as it beat faster and faster. And then it began to slow again and seemed better. I shrugged and walked a few feet closer to my table. I set the satchel down and placed each jar carefully on it, making sure the wax seal with the honeybee displayed perfectly to the others. Like the golden honey that glowed was not enough to know what was in the jar.

I rolled my eyes and carefully lined them up into a triangle to match my Mark and waited for the idiots to start swarming like the bees that they were, most of the time with stingers of their own. My Mark began to tingle again as I looked down the path and froze. An older, but familiar face, more matured and filled with tattoos, came walking toward me. My stomach sank as I recognized his tattoo and then groaned before running behind the strawberry farmer's animal skin hut and prayed to the old gods and new ones that Eric would not see me. I kneeled to the ground and tried to refocus my head. I looked down at my Mark and shook my head.

Was it the same Mark?

Chapter 13
Eric Greystone

It had been ten years since the shift of the planets had happened. I buried my parents and decided to take over the lands. I rebuilt Greystone land as my own and waited for the other families to return. I sent Mags and Jimmy away from the chaos of so much loss. They were not to come back to these lands. They were instructed by me and Oxana to find happiness, and we let them leave to do just that.

Mags was lucky that her mother had planned every outcome against Ragnar that day, including a spell embedded into the Labradorite necklace that Mags wore to keep her alive. Izzy had severed her link to her sister, but after several hours, Mags's eyes opened and her wound was healed. Jimmy had held her all night long, and at sunrise, she breathed again. The tears my brother shed were enough to send anyone into a sinking ship of sadness with him. We had just lost our parents, and for him to lose the love of his life was beyond reasoning as a young man. They lived with me for a few years until Oxana was able to finish the immortality spell.

We had pushed back a lot, knowing that it may not work. I also knew that if it did work, then eventually, I would have to bear the burden of finding the dagger and killing Ragnar. Selfishly, it was a wound that I was not ready to reopen yet. And with him gone for now, what was the rush in ending my life to destroy his? I had time. I was immortal now.

The world believed that our mother had performed it on us weeks before Ragnar tried to destroy our world, but in reality, it was her way of sending fear through anyone that tried to betray us to Ragnar. Ultimately, he had probably heard of it too, which sent him into his own madness of rage that night. He knew that we were too close to ending him.

As soon as the sun rose that next morning, and Mags was alive, Oxana's amulet began to glow and shake as the fire breathing dragon escaped the amulet and flew above us before landing on the ground. I grabbed my sword and was ready to fight for whatever was left of our lands and for my brother to live another day. Only, the dragon shrank and began to shapeshift back into a human form. Oxana appeared, and my jaw dropped as she stood naked in front of us, covered in ash and bruises. She covered herself with her hands as I dropped the sword and kept my eyes off of her nakedness. I walked over to her, taking my shirt off and covering her. She grabbed the shirt and tossed it over herself before assessing the damages. As

Jimmy ran and grabbed her a warm blanket that she gladly wrapped herself in.

"Ragnar?" she whispered with a hoarse voice.

I shook my head.

"Lady Cambridge?"

I shook my head.

"Izzy?"

I shook my head again.

"Oh, no… come here, sweet child." She pulled me toward her blanket-wrapped body and hugged me tight as the tears began to flow. "We will fix this. We will fix this all." She rubbed my shoulders and let me be a grieving child for once, pulling Jimmy into our embrace as we became the last standing folks left in Crystal Rock.

In ten years' time, I was no longer a child. Years of battles won. Ale drank to the bottom of barrels. Ladies to share as far as the eye could see. Today, however, was a day I always enjoyed sharing my own wealth with the townspeople to enjoy their sweets and delights. The town's market was open to all lands to join in the festivities of axe throwing, hair braiding, fire breathing dancers, sword swallowing idiots, fortune seers, and of course, the trades.

It was always my job to bring freshly hunted game in exchange for fresh strawberries from the old man farmer Finnian, who wouldn't have many years left. So, I lifted the branch over my shoulders with the squirrels tied evenly across it with twine as I made my way to the strawberry farmer who was usually next to Lenora's honey table or Gander's wood carvings.

I smiled when I saw him with my bowl ready for trade. I lifted the squirrels off my shoulders and handed them to him as his smile grew wide.

"Two bowls for this many, thank you. You know my fingers just don't hunt the way they used to." Finnian nodded and handed me an extra bowl of berries. I smiled and nodded as I lifted one and tried to toss it into my mouth but was bumped into by a female. I turned and watched, then my world stopped spinning.

Her long dark hair and goddess skin gleamed in the sunlight in a way that made me wonder if she was the true definition of beauty itself. I dropped the fresh strawberry that I had been ready to toss onto my tongue and watched her doe eyes meet mine in embarrassment as she dropped the furs she had been carrying with her. Her cheeks became red, mimicking the rose garden that had begun to bloom that I planted in remembrance of my mother. She smiled and apologetically knelt over and grabbed the strawberry that had dropped, wiping it and blowing the dirt off.

"I am so sorry—"

"No apologies needed. It was my own self that blocked you from your destination." I cleared my throat, and for the first time, I believed in love at first sight. I watched as her freckles along her nose made her seem even more innocent than anyone I had ever met before. I had been with many ladies over the years, but none have ever come close to the beauty that was standing in front of me. I wanted her, and not in a bedding way, but in a way that the old gods, the new gods, the sun, the moon had placed her in my path for a certain reason. She was meant for me. I knew it in the way my heart skipped a beat each time her eyes locked with mine.

She giggled and tossed the strawberry over her shoulder. "Honestly, I forgot where I was going."

I smiled and offered her a clean strawberry. She smiled and picked one, quickly tossing it onto her tongue and covering her mouth while she chewed it softly in front of me.

I grabbed her wrist gently and shook my head. "I am no one proper."

She smiled and nodded.

"Eric Greystone." I reached my hand out and waited for hers.

She tucked her hair behind her ear and blushed as she gave her hand to me. A slight tingle shot through my fingertips. I lifted it slowly and kissed the top of her hand. Her body shivered in the warmth of the season as she watched me carefully. I smirked as I knew she felt the tingling between us too.

"Aislynn! Where are you?" I heard a lady yell from across the way. The goddess of a woman in front of me turned quickly and giggled like a child as she turned back toward me. "Miss Meadows, come on now."

Meadows?

"I'm sorry, that's my mother, I must go." She smiled and held my grasp for a second longer. "It was nice to meet you… Eric."

I stared at her mother and tried to place where I had seen her before. Something about the name reminded me of someone. I shook my head and looked back at the goddess in front of me. I rubbed my thumb over her hand

before releasing it, nodding. "Likewise… Aislynn."
She blushed and turned to meet her mother. I watched as
the woman that was meant to be mine began to walk
away, and I knew that I couldn't let her go just yet. "Ais,
wait." I ran up to her and grabbed her torso gently.
"When will I see you again?"

She laughed and leaned into me, whispering in my
ear, "Meet me at sunset under the tree in the field atop
these bluffs. It's a full moon tonight, and I need to charge
my water, so I could use a warrior to protect me."

I didn't know if she was making a mockery of me or
if she truly needed the protection, but either way, I was
not going to pass up a moment with her. I prayed that she
meant it. I stared into her eyes and felt as if my soul was
meant for hers. I had never believed in love at first sight
until this very moment. I could feel my heart race, and I
watched as her gaze didn't break from mine. She has a
goodness about her, and all I wanted was to share in it
with her.

I nodded and smiled. "I will be there."

She laughed nervously and then winked before she
joined her mother, who began to lecture her about
walking away without warning.

I leaned against the barrel of leather that was waiting
to be traded next and smiled as I watched her make her
way through the crowd graciously. My fingers still
tingled with whatever magic she was filled with.

I want her. I need her. Forever.

I turned around and caught sight of the jars of honey.
I froze as I looked down at the arrangement that matched
my triangle Mark that had appeared after Oxana helped

with the immortality spell. A few years after my parents had died and Izzy had fled the lands, Oxana had found the runestone spell my father had been away to retrieve and decided to work on the ingredients. It took a few years for her to master the ingredients without them turning into a puff of smoke and a celestial event occurring before she tried the spell on my brother. When it seemed to work without any side effects, she did mine on the night of the solar eclipse. However, I ended up with a tattoo that seemed to randomly glow and burn. Instead of keeping it the skin tone color that it was, I tattooed it permanently onto my skin, tracing each triangle perfectly, and it never glowed again.

I looked at my forearm, then back down at the honey jars and huffed. "That's weird." I looked back at the farmer. "Hey, are you selling this honey too?"

He shook his head. "The young lady was just here a second ago." He scratched his head and looked up and down the rows. He shrugged. "Can't help you there."

I nodded and began to walk away.

14

Isadora Cambridge

I watched as he walked back down the path and wanted to bury myself into the bushes across the way for the rest of my life. I looked back down at my Mark and realized that something had happened, and fate was bringing us back together.

Why would we have the same Mark?

I left my honey stand and followed him at a distance, trying to get a closer look.

Would he even recognize me?

It had been so many years since we last saw each other. The last night we had together was unfortunately not a pleasant one. At least, for my sake, he was unconscious and did not see the worst parts of me. Or better, the worst parts of my father manipulating me—the weak parts of me.

I picked up my pace and watched as his broad shoulders carefully made their way through the overcrowded area. He was so careful to not bump into anyone. I watched as many ladies smiled and blushed as he passed and then began to whisper and giggle like stupid children. Even men stared and nodded toward him with an appreciation of his accomplishments.

Even though I had not seen him in ten years, I knew of his battles. He was Eric the Great. Eric, the warrior from the lands of Greystone. I wanted to be happy for him and what he achieved, but a part deep inside me was jealous that he didn't accomplish those things with me by his side. I could've been next to him as the first lady fighting battles and conquering the world.

I shook my head and watched as he began to slow his walk. I quickly mimicked him, turning to the table closest to me, and began to rummage through the handmade jewelry, stopping as the beautiful wire wrapped tourmaline stone fell flat into my hand and caught my attention even more than Eric had.

"That's two silvers. Do you want me to wrap it up for you, my lady?"

I jumped at the seller's voice and accidentally pulled the necklace from his wooden tree stand, snapping the branch that held the piece together.

"I am so, so sorry." My cheeks flushed as embarrassment claimed me.

He laughed and shook his head. "It's only a tree." He smiled. "Tell you what… You seem like you need a piece to hold close to your heart… Here." He smiled and took the tourmaline piece from my hand and began to wrap it in cloth. "Please, it's yours."

My blush deepened.

"You remind me of my late daughter. I would be honored to share the piece with you in honor of her."

I shook my head. "I could never. I just broke your stand, if anything I owe you three silvers." I reached into my satchel and grabbed the silver coins out and insisted on him taking them. "Please, for the damages that I've caused." If only he knew the amount of damages my past had already cost, then he would know the type of person I actually was. I didn't want to wear a piece of jewelry in honor of his late daughter, who was probably a fair lady who deserved better.

He smiled and shook his head. "It's yours, my lady. I will be offended otherwise."

The kindness I had felt from Lenora had been so undeserving that she would surely slit my throat in my sleep if she had known the world I had destroyed. I had killed my own sister, and for that, I would forever hold against my own self.

"You did what you needed to, Syphon. Your sister was an abomination to our power." My father's voice whispering made a shiver run through me, making me want to vomit.

"Shush," I whispered under my breath.

The seller had seemed to go unaware of the battle inside of my head as the demons fought between good and evil. I have always felt as though my mother was the good trying to battle my father's evil. But something inside of me screamed that she was long gone, while my father was rotting in that prison world she had placed him in.

I knew I needed to get him out of there, though. I needed to release him for my own sanity. It would be the only way he would finally leave me in peace with my own thoughts. Many nights he haunted my dreams as if I were standing face to face with him. He tried his damnedest to control me and plan my next move here on Earth. I needed to release him to clear my own head.

It was my own secret to bear, and I would never tell anyone of the hold he had on me. The world would burn me alive if they knew he lived on through me. They would think I would go mad, just as he had.

I just needed to find that damn Hildisvini dagger that had gone missing when I had awakened in the pile of ash, when our lands were destroyed and I was all alone.

I had thought that Eric and Jimmy were dead too until I had seen them down by the river weeks later, gathering buckets of water and carrying them back to the Greystone land. I watched the two of them from the trees and saw them join Oxana back at their home. Together they planted seeds and started crops to replenish the earth. I wanted to run to Eric and tell him how sorry I was for everything and tell him of my father's hold on me. But then I heard him. His words had haunted me and pushed me further away.

"She's dead, and she's not coming back," Eric had screamed at his brother. "Mother and Father are dead, and it's their fault. That family ruined ours, and all you want to do is find her. I never want to see them again." He spat to his side. "I'll kill her myself."

And that was the moment that I knew I needed to stay far away from him. The dagger was gone, my sister was gone, my parents gone, my lands gone, my friends were gone. Everything about my past was gone, and I needed to move forward and far away.

That was the first time that I heard my father's voice take over my head, and for the first time in weeks, my loneliness hadn't seemed so lonely.

"My sweetest child, we are not done yet. You need to release me from this place. We will take back what is ours. That Greystone family will get what's coming to them."

I grabbed my sword and headed far away.

"Here you go my lady," The seller handed me the tourmaline and nodded.

"Thank you. Really, thank you so much. This means a lot to me."

He smiled. "Glad I could help."

I smiled back and unwrapped the necklace before placing it over my head.

I turned and looked around for Eric, only to have lost him entirely. I exhaled slowly and headed back to my honey stand.

It wasn't meant to be.

"Probably for the better, Syphon," my father's voice reentered my thoughts.

I groaned and tried to hum a tune to make him disappear again.

"Izzy?" Eric's voice echoed behind me, and my entire body froze. I had expected to catch him by surprise, not the other way around. I wanted to turn around and see him up close, but I seemed to have lost all the courage I had a moment ago. I also knew that if I turned around now, then I would risk destroying his entire life with my father still looking for revenge against him and his family. If he ever became immortal, then my father would surely one day escape and find him. I swallowed hard, grabbed my tourmaline necklace, and ran far away from the market altogether.

Chapter 15
Eric Greystone

It was *her*.

I knew it was her.

I could feel her in my bones and my soul.

I wanted her to turn around and face me like the warrior she always said she was. I wanted to see the regret in her eyes from all the destruction she caused along with her psychotic father. I needed to hear the words escape her lips, see her sorrow for running away from everything instead of facing the pain with me. She was supposed to be my best friend, and instead of being there for me while I grieved my parents, she ran. She ran from everyone. I needed her to turn around to know of any sympathy that she still had inside her.

I *needed* to tell her that her sister was alive and that we were ready to kill her father in the prison world. I needed her to be on our side. I needed my friend back.

But instead, I watched as she ran away—again.

"Coward!" I yelled and regretted it the moment I said it. She stopped and began to turn before she clenched her fist and kept running.

I watched as she made her way through the crowd, and a part of me wanted to chase after her. I wanted to pin her against the cave wall and scream at her for leaving me to rebuild what her father destroyed. I also wanted to pull her in close and embrace her broken soul and save her from herself. I was torn as to what I wanted with her. I watched as her long blonde hair bounced with braids that were pinned perfectly in a pattern going down her back and her leather corset fit slim along her tunic. She was still Izzy, only a grown lady now. Every memory came flooding back to me in a whirlwind as I watched her go. I stood frozen, torn as to what I really needed to do. I was angry with her, but deep down, I always loved her as a friend, and I never wanted her to be in pain.

I saw Aislynn in the crowd coming back my way, and my heart began to race as her goddess beauty with soft eyes met mine. My heart told me to leave the past alone. If Izzy wanted to mend things, then she would. Now, at least I knew she wasn't too far away.

I inhaled slowly and watched as Izzy ran and quickly gathered honey jars from a table before heading for the bluffs.

I knew of the lady who made that honey. Lady Lenora tended the bees, and she was not far from here. I made a note to go to her home another day and see if I could talk to Izzy.

I turned just as Aislynn was at my side, I gently grabbed her hand and kissed it. "Ah, we meet again. May I interest you in a dance?" I looked back at her mother and waited for permission.

Aislynn smiled as her cheeks reddened. Her mother smiled and nodded, releasing her of her duties for the night.

"Thank you." I grabbed her hand and lifted it high as we made our way through the crowd to the fiddler.

The moon began to rise as we drank ale and counted the stars. Hours had passed, and Aislynn had decided to stay later than she was meant to with a promise for me to bring her to her front door safely.

"Why have I never seen you before?" I asked, as we laid next to one another across from the trade show, the fiddler still playing in the distance. But my legs were too weak to dance any longer, and instead, we left the laughter of the dancers to play as background music to our ears.

She giggled. "I have been near this place my whole life." She sat up and pointed toward my land and squinted. "Over there. I grew up close to those lands, but there was a tragedy that brought my mother and I further away."

I sat up and let my smile dull as I knew the exact night. I nodded and grabbed her hand, interlocking her fingers with mine. She leaned closer to me and laid our hands on my chest. She closed her eyes and seemed in deep thought. Her warmth, or maybe it was the bottomless ale we had consumed, but something about her closeness made my world a little brighter. I memorized her features and wanted to dream of her tonight and from this day forward.

"You have a strong heart." She smiled, opening her eyes. "The heart of a warrior."

I laughed and brought her hand to my lips, kissing it gently. "Warriors do not have hearts. Anyone with a heart wouldn't fight in wars."

She shook her head. "You fight for love. Your heart is pure, and the rhythm is exceptionally beautiful." She swallowed hard. "May I?" she asked, as she grabbed my palm and began to examine it.

I nodded. "Not much to see."

"You have had much grief in your life, but you always overcome it." She leaned in closer and then looked back at me with concern. "You should have a long life, unexpectedly longer than most. Marriage that is true and everlasting. Hmm…" She giggled and continued, "A child…" I sat up, intrigued, and waited. But she froze as her eyes widened. She quickly set my hand down and shook her head. "I think the ale is beginning to cloud my reading."

"No, keep going. I want to hear your words."

She shook her head. "I lost my train of thought. It's getting much too dark to see clearly." She smiled and laid her head against my chest. I wrapped my arm around her and began to lay back with her in my arms.

"We should be going soon," she whispered sleepily.

I inhaled her scent of lavender and lilies and always wanted to remember it. "Say the word, and I will get you home."

"Maybe a little longer." She said softly.

I nodded and held her close. My heart felt whole for the first time in a long time, and if this was what my mother had always talked about with my father, then I finally understood it. Aislynn was the one that I wanted to spend forever with. She was going to be mine. My heart had been searching for healing, and with her by my side, she was exactly who I had been looking for. She was different from all others.

"Hey, Ais…" Her breathing became even as she rested her eyes next to me.

"Yes?" she whispered.

I lost the courage and decided to let fate decide if we were meant to be together.

I looked down at her and watched her peacefully sleeping. I carefully sat up without moving her too much and lifted her into my arms to walk her home. Her small frame fit perfectly in my arms, and each step that I took closer to her home made me want to slow down even more. I wanted to have every moment possible with her. I wanted her to be mine more than anyone I had ever had before. Before her, it was as though nothing in my past ever mattered. She was going to be the one to love me the way I had never believed was even possible.

She began to stir as we reached sight of her home, and I looked down at her one last time as I began to make my way down the hill.

"Don't leave yet."

I stopped walking and looked down at her.

Her eyes slowly opened as she looked around at our surroundings. "You weren't supposed to leave the hill yet."

I laughed and set her down gently, holding her until she regained her balance.

She smiled and fixed her long black hair, tucking it gently behind her ear and blushing. "I wasn't done with you yet." She blushed as she wrapped her arms slowly around my neck and stretched up on her toes.

I felt my heart race as I lifted her into my arms and wrapped her legs around me, letting her lips find mine and finally following my heart.

She was going to be mine and I, hers.

Forever.

16

Isadora Cambridge

It had been months since I had seen Eric at the market. Spring was here after a long and cold winter. We were lucky to have saved the bees through the freezes that mother nature had been playing hard against us. I felt relieved knowing that Eric had never come looking for me. Hopefully, he was too busy and forgot about me. It was bad enough that he knew I was alive. Then to call me a coward at the market in front of everyone… I wanted to turn around and face him. I wanted to tell him of my father taking over my actions that night, but I knew that he wouldn't believe me. I knew that he would only think of me as weak for not keeping him out of my head. So, instead of facing my friend who now hates me, I ran.

With the warm weather finally letting us venture out again and the flowers beginning to bloom, I decided it was time to head to the river. My father's voice had been quiet for weeks now, and I prayed that he had finally left me for good. It was time to make the grave I had been wanting to do for years for my sister and my mother. I needed to find the perfect shells to place at their headstones.

I needed to stop running and finally settle here. The bees were beginning to trust me and not sting me as often, and with Lenora growing elderly, she wanted someone to pass along her honest business to. She had never married or had children. She was a loner, just like me.

"I'm heading to the river. Do you need me to stop for anything else?" I asked Lenora, as I grabbed my satchel and headed toward the door.

She smiled and shook her head. "Enjoy, sweet one."

I smiled and nodded.

The last decade had been a quiet one physically. It was more so mentally that wouldn't shut the hell up. Lenora never asked me of my past. She took me in and had me help her around her home for payment of staying. She never talked of her past, either. We seemed to have an understanding that neither of us wanted to relive those lives. We spent most nights eating dinner together, but other than that, she seemed perfectly busy with her bees and garden, and I spent my days adventuring in the forest and trying to keep my father silent.

Over the last few years, I began to use my elemental magic again, always in hopes that it would spark my syphoning back, but truly, I didn't want it back after what I had done to my own sister. Though, a part of me felt that if I could get my syphoning back, I could bring my sister back. Somehow reverse time itself and start over. I felt drawn to thyme and continued to try multiple spells with it. But unfortunately, there always seemed to be an ingredient missing.

The river was calmer than I had expected. The snow had finally melted, and the sand was full of shells washed up from the shore. I smiled as I took my boots off and let the sand wiggle between my toes. I lifted my satchel over my head and laid it on the ground. Stretching high in the sky and letting the sun warm my cheeks in the spring air, I sat down and listened to the river flowing. There was something about the rhythmic pattern that made me feel at home.

I raised my palm and called the river to me. I watched as the water twirled in a circular motion and bounced to me. It shimmered in the sunlight and then I let it flow around me, calling the river to flow in a dancing motion. I smiled as I remembered doing this silly childish magic with my sister years ago.

I swallowed hard and threw my palm down, letting the water crash, forming a circle around me.

"All my fault." I shook my head. "Stupid syphoning. Mags, I wish you were still here."

I stood and began to search the beach for shells and stones to place at their empty graves. I watched as a longship came into view and began to come closer to the shore. The river was wide, but I could see a man and woman with a hood covering her face on the ship pointing toward Greystone landing. I grabbed my satchel and ran behind the trees. I watched carefully as the woman pulled her hood further over her face and sat back down on the wooden plank. Then, I saw the man turn in my direction, and I stood, frozen.

It was Eric's brother coming home.

It had been years since he'd been home. I squinted to verify it was really him and couldn't believe it myself. It must be a special occasion?

Jimmy had disappeared when I had. I had gone back one time and saw him packing bags for a long journey. I didn't blame him for leaving. I was actually surprised that Eric had stayed. None of us should've stayed on that land after the massacre that happened there. I had laid flowers at their parents' grave one time, and after that, I never went back. I watched as Eric hugged his brother at the headstone and decided that would be my last memory of them.

I swallowed hard and held my breath, praying that he and his lady never saw me.

Good for him, I thought. *He finally married someone.* I wasn't sure if he would ever get over losing Mags. I watched as the longship passed and then walked back out on the beach. I began to rummage through the shells for the perfect one. I picked through nearly a hundred of them before I finally found two perfectly shaped heart stones and the most unique river rocks that I could find.

I examined them both closely and smiled. I placed them carefully in my satchel and began to walk away from the river. I stopped in my tracks as I looked down and saw a stone staring back at me.

I bent down and picked up the small hagstone and laughed at how the world had a funny way of letting fate decide. I lifted it and held it up against the sun. A small hole in the shape of a heart let the sunlight beam through it.

"A magical hagstone," I said while looking through it. "Thanks, Mother." I winked at the sky and placed it carefully in my pocket, keeping it clenched tightly in my fist. It had been the first hagstone I had seen in a decade, and to finally find one while not even searching for one, I knew it was meant for me. It was a small reward, letting me know that I was on the right track. I was healing, and for the first time in a decade, I felt as if my mother and sister were with me today on my beach walk.

I nodded and smiled to myself.

I made my way back home and walked behind the house to the spot where the sun touched the ground from sunrise to set. Lenora walked out next to me as I dug a small area out and began to plant the Garden Angelica that she had picked out for me in memory of them. I placed the plant and pushed the soil down firmly around it. I admired the whimsical little white puff balls and stood, stepping back to see them glisten in the sun.

I turned to Lenora and smiled. "That's perfect."

She nodded and rubbed my shoulder gently before turning and going back into the house. She was beginning to slow down in life, and I was sad to think that I would have to add another Garden Angelica to this area sooner than later. But today was a day of celebration and not death. I needed to push that thought deep down and let fate decide.

I opened my satchel and pulled the two heart shaped stones and shells from it and placed them carefully under the plant.

"Mother and Mags… I miss you more than you will ever know. I wish things had been different." I swallowed hard and wiped a tear that began to fall. "If I could've saved you both, I would have. May you both rest easy, and I hope to see you both in Valhalla one day."

I hugged myself and waited for the moment of sadness to disappear.

"Stupid girl. Your mother is not dead." My father's voice interrupted my thoughts, and I felt his sickness creeping back into me with a hold that made me want to rip my skin off. *"She is here with me in this prison."* He laughed, which sent a shiver down my spine. *"I will continue to torture her until you release me from this hell. Find a way, or she will die here alone and never be able to reach Valhalla."*

My body froze as I looked around and wanted to believe that I was making up scenarios and that his voice was never real to begin with. But then I felt it. I felt his thoughts trying to control my body.

"Yes, Syphon, I am getting stronger here. I need more. More witches, I need their souls to feed on. The Greystones' power has faded, and I want more. Find the dagger, and kill more witches with it."

I felt a wave of nausea consume me. My body shuddered as I ran over to the fence post and vomited ferociously over it.

"Get out of my head," I yelled, as I wiped my mouth with the back of my hand.

"I am only getting stronger." I could see the smirk across his face as if he were standing in front of me. *"You are mine to control now. Find that dagger, and consume more souls. One of those pitiful lives will have to open the door to leave this place."*

My mother's words flooded my memory as she told me only a child of my descent would unlock that world. I didn't want him out, he had destroyed too many lives and would only destroy more. But then I thought of my mother. What if she was really trapped there? What if she was still alive and I could save her?

My throat began to fill with more acid as bile grew again. I braced myself as I vomited more.

Lenora came running toward me as fast as her fragile legs could bring her. She placed my arm across her shoulder and hobbled us slowly back into her home. She laid me down on my bed and grabbed a pail, placing it beside me. She quickly went to the kitchen and began to brew some tea over the fire.

My father's voice grew louder as he screamed at me. I felt as if he would never stop and plugged my ears as I began to scream, trying to drown him out. Lenora turned around and looked back at me with saddened eyes as she reached me. She placed her hands over my hands and tried to drown the voices with me.

"He's back, isn't he? Ragnar?" She yelled.

My eyes widened with shock. I thought I had hid my secret so well. I nodded with tears in my eyes as the nausea grew again and my screams began, hoping to stop the pain he was causing inside of my head. A migraine that was surely going to pop my blood vessels and kill me by sundown. My head felt as if it were ready to explode as his voice screamed at me.

"Get up, Syphon! Get up and find the dagger!"

His voice boomed through me, rattling in my head.

"Find the dagger!"

It seemed to echo in all of Crystal Rock.

"Find the dagger!"

I could feel it vibrating all the way to Greystone land and felt sick.

I closed my eyes and tried to let the screams of both my father and I consume me. Lenora laid down next to me and kept her hands on mine and held me close, trying to comfort me the only way she could. I could feel her body trying to transfer whatever magic she had left in her to me, and I knew I was undeserving of it. I tried to keep my wall up and keep her out. Her elderly body continued for hours as she embraced me. It was exhausting trying to keep everyone out of my head.

I had not felt close to anyone other than her in a decade. I tried to place where she would've known my secret from and if she knew me as a child, but nothing seemed to make sense. My head was spinning, and I just needed to close my eyes and forget about this world. I needed to die. I needed to end this torture for good. My father would have no other way of communicating with this world if I left it. I squeezed my eyes shut tighter and let the darkness consume me.

I woke in silence. My eyes slowly opened and looked around the room. The fire from the kitchen was nothing but ashes now, smoking lightly as the untouched tea sat in the pot. I turned to see Lenora still lying next to me. She was sleeping peacefully, and I quietly stood up and made my way to the fire and relit the kindle to try and salvage the concoction.

"When did it start again?"

I was startled when Lenora spoke. I turned quickly and held my chest, breathing heavily as she sat up slowly. Her fragile body was weakening by the hour. I grabbed a wooden spoon and stirred the tea a few times while the boiling began.

I shook my head and kept my mouth shut.

"I knew your mother." She exhaled slowly. "She asked me days before she passed to look out for you girls."

I stared at her in disbelief.

"Oxana explained to me what had happened with your sister and mother. She had said you went missing." She folded her hands across her lap. "To find you and protect you was my last purpose in life… I was no good of a person, and I needed one last good deed in this life to try and make things right." She half smiled. "I wanted to help you. I thought he had finally left you alone. I was finally at peace that he had left you alone." She tried to stand, but her arms shook as she tried to lift her own weight before falling back down onto the bed. She waved

her hands as I tried to come and help her. "Tea please."
She repositioned herself onto the bed and leaned against
the wall as comfortably as she could as I handed her a
mug of the steaming liquid. I added her honey to the tea
and stirred it for her. She smiled and breathed in the
steam. "Thank you."

I nodded, still stunned. I had never heard her speak
so many words in the years that I had spent with her.

"Today is my last day here. I am out of time, and I
am so sorry that I was not able to get rid of that monster
within your head." She sipped her tea slowly.

I shook my head. "I was never yours to heal." I could
feel my throat getting tighter as I tried to swallow my
tears. Time was never on my side. No matter the lengths
of my life, time was the one thing always running against
me. I cursed it as I inhaled heavily.

She looked back at me and nodded. "That Hildisvini
dagger should've been destroyed."

My eyes widened as she spoke of the long lost
object.

"You need to destroy it. I had hoped to find a way to
help your mother, but it is an impossible task. You must
destroy the dagger and live free from his hold on you."

"That dagger is long gone. It disappeared that
night."

She shook her head. "No, sweet one. The Meadows
must still have the dagger. You can hate them for that one
if you would like."

I shook my head. "I don't unders—"

"The Meadows have the dagger. They were to keep it
far away from you. They should've sunk it to the bottom

of the river, but something tells me it has made its way back to these lands recently, and someone is using it for you to have that kind of episode again. Blood magic is being performed for him to be gaining power over you like that. The closer your father is to you, or his imprisonment cursed dagger, then the more of a hold he has on you. You were doing so good child." She shook her head and sipped her tea again. "That Jasper stone was given to another family. Between the Hildisvini dagger and the Jasper stone, they contain power that can be used for good or evil, and they should both be destroyed. No amount of power is worth the dangers that they can cause. You must find them both and destroy them." She handed me her mug with shaky hands and leaned her head on my shoulder. "Isadora, you must destroy those objects so your father can never touch his chaos power again, promise me."

I felt as if my throat was a desert, and I had no voice at all.

"That was the best tea yet." She smiled.

I nodded, not really understanding. I laid my head upon hers and kissed her hair gently as I listened to her take her last breath next to me. I inhaled and let my chest rattle as I tried to process everything at once.

Lenora, the lady that took me in and helped me for the last few years, was the last person I had in this world helping me, and now she was gone too.

I wished I would've told her the love I held for her. I wish I would've been able to spend the years knowing her past more and not hiding so much. I wish I had known that she knew my mother. I wished that she knew how much I cared for her.

I sniffled hard and gently laid her down on the bed. I carefully placed her hands crossed over her chest, and touching her hands for another minute to send my love through to her, I prayed that she was at peace and could feel my gratitude. I breathed in and nodded as I looked at her one more time before walking outside and digging another hole, only this time it was a much larger one and needed a headstone and Garden Angelica planted with her as well. It was supposed to be a happy day, but instead, it turned into another loss. Again, I was alone.

"Alone?" my father's voice echoed in the distance. *"You are never alone."*

I knew what I needed to do now. I needed to destroy the Hildisvini dagger, and I needed to find the Jasper stone. I needed to destroy them for Lenora and for my own sanity. Maybe if I fulfilled her wish, I could be forgiven by the old gods, and maybe, just maybe, I could see my sister and mother again in Valhalla.

Chapter 17
Eric Greystone

I was going to make her my wife in a few short days. Frigga's day was the only true day to be married to have the goddess bless our marriage with love and high fertility for our future. We would need heirs to continue our story and let us have the true love that everyone would dream of. The ceremony was to remain small, unlike traditional weddings at nearby villages. Our lands were not going to be able to accommodate shelter for all villages to join us. Our wedding was to be the first of Greystone land in a decade. But without my parents, there weren't many others that I wanted to attend. Oxana would surely be with us, and my brother promised to join me in the sword ceremony.

He and Mags were not planning on staying much longer. Neither of them said it, but I knew that they were getting nervous about Izzy finding her sister alive, and who was to say what was going on in Izzy's head these days.

Would she try to kill her again?

We didn't want to find out.

Aislynn's mother assured me that she would be able to put a glamour spell on Mags to keep her out of sight for the rest of the week. It was a big task that would surely weaken the mother of the bride. But we could not have Izzy coming around and seeing her sister alive. I wanted to believe Izzy was good, but there was no knowing what she had been up to over the last decade without talking to her. She had made it very clear that she wanted to stay far away the day of the market.

With talk of our wedding, the villages were sailing up and down the river to bear us with gifts and short stays to celebrate and ask for protection from invaders. Word of my previous battles had soared across the lands, and many wanted me on their side. But there were still others that wanted to conquer our lands and make them their own. We had made our way to a few villages to announce our families joining swords, and many seemed pleased. My men that sailed with me were the only ones skeptical of Aislynn joining the longship with us. They deemed an unwed pagan to be bad luck on the waters. My men wanted us to marry sooner or leave her home from now on. She found a way to track me from the long nights away with small blood magic. Her map was enchanted with old magic, and with a little drop of my blood, it let her follow me along the river. It gave her peace of mind while I was away.

She was to exchange swords with me the night of our ceremony. She already had a dagger she had been waiting to gift me in exchange for protection in both love and war. She had my heart fully, and I would gladly give her anything she wanted. It was the only time I had wished that I had kept that sword from Izzy. I hadn't dared to go and find her at the honey house, but something about that sword made me wish that I had it for my future wife to be able to pass down to our children. We were eager to grow our family right away. I had never given much thought to being a father, but I hoped that I was half as decent as my own was. Being an immortal meant that my child would age and one day die. I wished that we could recreate the immortality spell and give my strong children the choice of forever. But that would be another conversation with Aislynn in the future.

I had to go to the market today. A well-known jeweler made Aislynn the most elegant ring twisted with twigs and leaves of silver and rose gold. I had him bless the ring on the river and pray to the goddess of family and fertility. The jeweler said that it was his most intricate piece he had done in years, and it would surely be one of a kind as he would not be able to recreate the fine piece again.

Aislynn had planned to exchange rings and the swords and asked me to bring her dagger to the swordsmith to sharpen and clean. She had made me promise not to take it out of the cloth, and she swore from her pagan practice that it was bad luck to see it before the ceremony. I, of course, rolled my eyes and told her it was a myth. But she was persistent on superstitions.

The sun was warm as I began the journey back to the market. I knew I needed to keep the trip short and be back to finish clearing the walkway to the arbor for this weekend. I nodded and smiled at each trader as I made my way through. I came to the end of the market, only to be disappointed as I glanced at each table with hope of seeing the honey stand. I knew I shouldn't have been looking, but a part of me wanted to clear the air before I wed Aislynn.

I need to see her.

I needed to know she was okay.

Last night a dream came to me. Ragnar's mother appeared to me in her ghostlike form. I had not seen her in ages. She begged me to help the broken one. I tried to shake her off and get her away from me, but even when I opened my eyes, she was still standing in front of me. I had looked over to Aislynn, as she laid her head peacefully, sound asleep and oblivious to the woman, and for the first time in my life… *I* was afraid. Not for myself, but what she may do to my love if I didn't obey her.

I sat in bed awake the rest of the night and waited until sunrise to head to the market. I didn't know what I was meant to do, but I knew I needed to at least talk to her. With a decade between us, I didn't even know her anymore. And maybe that was for the best.

Then, I saw the honey stand hidden behind the swordsmith's tent. I peered closer and agreed that today was the day. I was going to talk to Izzy whether she wanted to or not.

I took a sharp left and walked behind the people, where extra stock sat in wooden crates. I quickly snuck up behind her. She couldn't get far this time, even if she wanted to.

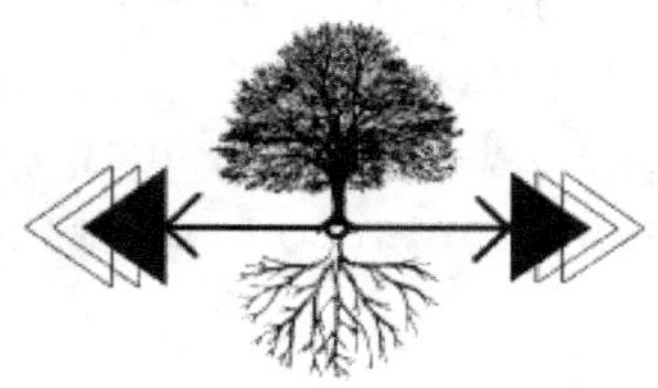

Izzy stood behind the table, fumbling with the jars and organizing them into a triangle again. I glanced down at my Mark and moved closer behind her.

"Izzy… Don't run," I whispered.

I watched carefully as her body tensed. She stopped moving the jars and straightened herself. She peered to her left and then right and realized that she was trapped.

"Please," I whispered, as I got an arm's length away from her.

Just as I reached her and tried to make her face me, she grasped a jar and turned quickly, chucking the heavy jar toward my skull.

My eyes widened with shock as I dodged it. She turned to grab another one, but it was just enough of a pause that I could see her eyes were swollen and red. My heart sank as my entire childhood resurfaced, and every memory we had shared together came crashing back into me like the waves on the river. I knew I had failed her. I knew that the ghost lady was angry with me for abandoning the broken one when she needed help. I knew I had ruined her.

But it was too late. She chucked the jar and hit me straight in the stomach, just enough to knock me off my guard and keel over. The jar exploded, and I was covered in sticky honey and shards of glass. I wouldn't have cared much, except that when I went to wipe the liquid gold off, my hand was covered with honey and blood.

I looked back up at Izzy, her eyes in shock as she shook nervously before running past me.

I sucked in a breath and grabbed an animal hide from the vendor next to her stand. "I'll pay you back." I pressed it hard against my abdomen and ran after her.

Isadora Cambridge

I ran until my lungs were ready to explode, gasping for air as I made it to the field. I ran to the lone tree and let my knees buckle under me. Hugging the tree for leverage before sinking to the field, my chest burned as my emotions swarmed me. I couldn't handle any more pain today. And as much as I didn't want to admit it… I wanted to be near him.

"Greystone… I despise that family. Kill him."

"No," I yelled at his voice that wouldn't leave me the fuck alone. "Stay away from him."

"Iz… It's just me." Eric inhaled sharply. "Please let me talk to you." His voice was already too close to me as I opened my eyes.

"Leave me alone." I sat up and pushed him further away from me. "Get away from me. Far away."

He grabbed my wrists and pinned my back against the tree without showing mercy.

He's going to kill me.

The back of my head hit the bark, and I prayed that it would end swiftly or at least silence my father's voice for a while.

"Just kill me," I screamed into his face, as my world crumbled. "I know it's what you've wanted."

His body stiffened as he loosened his grip on my wrists before pounding the tree behind me, next to my ears. I jumped as the bark crumbled and fell to my knees as he panted in front of me.

"Kill you?" he breathed heavily. "For the sake of the gods, I've looked for you for years to save you from yourself." He stepped back and wiped the sweat from his brows as I winced.

I watched as drops of blood began to form on the ground next to him.

I gasped as I stood and ran to him. "Sit." I grabbed his arm and tried to pull him down, but he refused. "You're bleeding."

He scoffed and ripped his arm from mine. "Because of you." He half laughed and looked down at the wound. "It'll scar by sundown."

I stared at the open gape and watched it begin to glow as it began to slowly close.

He pointed to the self-healing wound and smirked. "Immortal… remember?"

"You did it?" I stepped back and watched him carefully. "I thought your mother…"

His gaze met mine, and I could see the pain the words held deep within him.

"Never mind." I shook my head.

He exhaled heavily and sat down under the tree. "Can you please stop running for a second?" He pointed to the space next to him and waited.

Defeated, I sat.

I could feel something between us as the silence became deafening.

"I'm to marry in a few days." His voice stated as if not a day had passed between us.

I nodded. "I heard."

He laughed, and instead of saying anything more, I just laughed with him. I didn't know what it was about him, but I felt safe sitting with him. Maybe he wasn't going to kill me after all. I looked back at him and studied his face.

"You still look like you."

He turned and smiled. "You look…" He turned back away and inhaled slowly. "You look grown." He nodded and turned back at me.

I watched as his eyes locked onto my forearm. Shock filled as he grabbed my wrist, pulling it against his.

"When did you get this?" he asked, as he placed his arm next to mine.

I swallowed hard as I compared the identical Marks and shook my head. "I don't know, a few years ago." I shrugged and pulled my arm back. "What does it mean?"

He shook his head and stared back at his Mark. "Mine appeared the night I turned immortal." He stood up and paced back and forth. "A few years ago."

I jumped up and examined his, noting the ink that was used to trace the lines of the triangles. "Mine isn't dark like this… I don't understand it."

He rubbed his Mark. "I didn't want others to question it, so I made it permanent."

I nodded.

"Are you immortal too?"

I laughed. "I sure hope not. This life sucks." I covered my mouth after letting the words escape. "I'm sorry… I didn't mean that."

"Yes, you did." He walked closer to me.

I stepped back out of the habit of not wanting anyone near me.

"Iz, would you stop walking away from me?" He shook his head. "Damn. I came to find you. Are you okay?"

I stopped walking and stared back at him, confused. "You came to check on me?" I shook my head. "I thought you hated me."

"Hate you? No." He walked closer. "I looked for you for a year after everything happened… It was like you disappeared. I thought you were dead." He closed his eyes. "You were my friend, and I left you alone. What kind of warrior does that make me?" He opened his eyes, and they glistened in the sun. "I gave my word to my mother that I would protect you… and I have not only failed you, but her as well. I should've kept searching for you to make sure you were safe… It was my job to keep —"

I scoffed. "You didn't fail, because I am no one's *job*." I turned and began to march away, but he grabbed my wrist and pinned me against the lone tree that we had grown up around. And before I knew it, he had the back of my head and pulled me against him, breathing heavily.

He seemed conflicted, but something about his closeness made me want him more. I could feel the tension growing between us. His eyes locked with mine as I tried to squirm away from him, only to hope that he didn't release me.

His jaw tightened and brows furrowed. I wasn't sure if he was going to kill me or kiss me. I shook like a coward under him and prayed that his lips would graze mine. I didn't know what love was, and I had never let a man close enough to breathe against me… Until now.

He groaned as his lips crushed mine.

My soul seemed to awaken with an explosion in my own world. My forearm began to tingle and then burn. His lips pulled back slowly as he looked down. Both of our Marks were illuminating between us.

Something inside me felt stronger. Something about his closeness made me feel whole.

"Eric…"

His eyes met mine with worry. "Izzy…"

Our gaze locked on one another as every emotion from our past finally caught up to us. I let his lips trail down my neck and my tunic before I pulled him back to my lips, our tongues colliding as his warmth made me feel safe.

We both stopped at the same time, breathing heavily, as I pulled his head into my chest. I lifted it back up to see his features conflicted. I pulled him hard against me and hugged him tight as the tears began to flow. He wrapped his arms around me and caressed my braids, comforting me. He gently set me back on my feet and lifted my chin to him.

"Kill him," my father whispered.

I didn't want to ruin the moment, but I knew as much as I wanted this feeling to last, he was not meant to be mine anymore. The gods played a cruel game with me as they had done for years, and now to give him a matching Mark as mine… We were not meant to be together. We were meant to run from one another—for my short lifetime anyway.

"I have to go," I whispered, wanting to leave him with his dignity still intact for his wife-to-be. But he shook his head.

"Can we just talk? Give me ten minutes. A minute per year we missed. Please, Iz?" he pleaded, not letting me pass him.

I looked into his emerald eyes and felt the control he had over me begin to grow.

"Control?" I could hear my father chuckle. *"No, I have all the control, Syphon. Not this weak Greystone."*

I wanted to shake him out of it, but I just sat quietly, trying to seem normal to the eye.

"Ten minutes," I agreed.

I smiled and was thankful for the extra time, even though I knew it was wrong. With the pain of losing Lenora, though, I could use a friend for a little while.

Ten minutes turned into hours as the sun began to set. He told me about how he rebuilt the lands after the chaos and how Oxana lived and had a deeper secret as a shapeshifter.

"I had always thought that I had made it all up in my head." We both laughed.

He explained how Oxana was able to help with the immortality spell, but that it hurt like a son of a bastard. It did not turn out how Jimmy's had, and he had never figured it out why. He said that he wondered if the universe somehow fated us to meet again by sharing a Mark. We had not figured it out. But it was truly odd that my sister shared a lifeline with me, and now he and I shared a Mark. It made us both wonder if we had some kind of link to one another.

Neither of us knew what any of it truly meant. But maybe in time we would.

"I'm going to wed in a few days' time."

The words froze me again, knowing that if life went the way it was supposed to, he would have been mine. A pain in my heart grew as I thought of the future that we could have had, but instead, I ruined it for us and sealed a fate of loneliness for myself.

"Does she make you happy?" I swallowed hard.

He looked out toward the field and smiled. "She really does."

I smiled sadly. "Good. Then, I am happy for you."

I grabbed his hand and interlocked my fingers with his, holding them in the air. "Eric, the greatest warrior to live and now the ugliest husband to be to the poor soul that's willing to put up with your shit."

We laughed as if a natural friendship had never left us.

I waited for him to bring up my sister, but he never did. A part of me wanted to talk about it, maybe to clear the air as to what actually happened that night. I knew I woke up with blood on my hands, but it wasn't my choice. I wished I could tell him that, but I was too cowardly to bring her name up.

"Hey, Iz…"

I looked back at him and felt the pain in my heart grow as I knew we were coming to an end. Soon, I would be back at Lenora's empty home.

He seemed conflicted as to what he wanted to say next. He shook his head and swallowed hard.

I looked away, knowing that I deserved the loneliness and I shouldn't be selfish in wanting to keep him to myself. Plus, my father's voice would haunt me for a lifetime, and I could never bring Eric back into my world and torture him again with my family's drama. I could never take his happiness away again.

"You have to go?" I whispered.

He cleared his throat. "I actually was supposed to drop this off with the swordsmith to polish it." He pulled a small sword covered in cloth from his sheath. "The sword to exchange with Aislynn."

"Aislynn?" My brain began to buzz. "That sounds so familiar."

He laughed. "We met their family as children, I guess. At least, that's what her mother told me. I truly don't recall." He shrugged.

"Huh." I shrugged. "I guess you two were fated from the beginning."

His smile faded as he looked back at me. "I'm sorry. I know we were told that we would hold a future together as kids, but then so much happened, and you were gone for so long. I… I… Izzy, I really do love her."

I pushed a smile through, even though I wanted to cry.

"We will take her out of this world. He is yours to control."

I closed my eyes and tried to ignore my father's voice.

"I'm happy for you. I am."

He half smiled. "Our kiss—"

I covered his mouth. "Don't."

His brows furrowed as he peeled my fingers off his mouth.

"Our kiss is not regretted." He smirked. "It was long overdue. You will always be a part of me, and that kiss will stay with me always. That kiss was an apology for leaving you alone." He swallowed hard. "You are never alone, and you are always welcome back to our lands."

Our lands. I could feel my cheeks redden with excitement, but then I thought of all the bad things I had done—and would do—if I stayed too close to him.

If only he actually knew that I was never fully on my own, then he would think differently of me.

I smiled and nodded. "Friends?" I spit in my hand and held it out for him.

He smiled. "Friends." And there the pact was, and there it would stay.

He stood and pulled me up with him. "I really have to get back to the market before the swordsmith leaves. Ais will kill me."

I laughed. "Yeah, I need to grab the leftover honey jars unless the thieves stole them."

He shook his head and lifted his shirt, showing me the scar that had formed over the hours we had spent together. "That's a scar that will stay year round, and now I'm going to need a full jar of that honey before I head back home as your apology."

I smirked and nodded as we began to walk back to the market.

He lifted his sheath over his head to place the blade back in it, but the cloth unfolded and the jagged dagger fell out. It landed on the ground, sending a quake through the entire field, and a forcefield exploded between him and I, sending us both in opposite directions as the breath from my lungs escaped, biting my lip on my way down to the rugged ground. I could taste the blood as I stood and searched my surroundings.

What the hell was that?

"My dagger!" my father's voice screamed. *"Get my dagger. Get me out of here now, Syphon. Kill him. Free me!"*

I let my eyes refocus as I watched Eric bend down and pick up the Hildisvini dagger. His grasp shook heavily as he began to curse at the dagger. "Ignis," he yelled, as his fists became flames, and his rage came through them.

I ran to him and yelled, "Aqua." letting the cooling mist extinguish the flames as his hands shook uncontrollably underneath mine.

My brain began to rapid fire. "Meadows," I whispered. "Aislynn Meadows. That's your wife-to-be."

I looked up from the dagger.

He was back at me with disbelief and nodded.

As if we were thrown back in time, the field began to spin and then disappeared as the night that we both tried to forget came back into view.

We watched the dagger get handed over to my mother by Lady Meadows. The hagstone slipped into my mother's pocket next to the dagger. The Jasper stone ignited magic for my father. The entire night replayed in ways that half of it I did not remember. My mother grasped a black liquid in her other hand as she held it close to her chest and prayed to the gods for strength to protect her family. There was no way that I had seen it all and not done anything differently to save everyone. We watched his parents... And then there she was... Mags... Lifeless in my arms.

A blood curdling scream escaped both of our throats as we were thrown back into our world, and the field came back in view with the sun setting behind us.

"Just go," I screamed. "Get away from me!"

Eric shook his head. "Stop!"

"Get away," I screamed, and instead of letting him take another step, I pulled my sword from my back and pointed it at him. The sword that I had won with dragon's blood now threatened his life. "Get that thing away from me. Get away from me." The tears flowed. "Please, just get it away from me." I tried to wipe my tears with shaking hands as the sword felt too heavy for my own arms. The weight of the world was back on me. "Please," I begged.

"No! Take it. Free me." My father's voice demanded.

"Please, Eric. Keep it away from me."

He swallowed hard as he knelt down to grab the dagger again and seemed in pain as he had to touch the weapon that ended his parents life all over again. A burden that he had been carrying with him all day without knowing. A weapon that had been in his home unknowingly for months. A dagger that held too many secrets for either of us to want to keep.

He nodded slowly and wrapped it back in the cloth before turning and walking back to his lands, opposite the direction of the market. I sucked in a breath and tried to clear my thoughts.

"Stupid, Syphon. If you won't take it from him, then I will do it for you."

"Leave me alone," I screamed and fell to the ground, covering my ears. I didn't dare to see if Eric had seen me go mad before he left me alone. I just prayed that he had been far enough away before I finally broke.

"I will give you everything you want… You want Eric? You want power? You want your family back? I will give you it all. Just let me in, Syphon. Let me make life easy for you for a while. I can help you live the life you

want. A husband, a child, a family. I can help you get everything you desire in your lonely, pitiful world."

His voice echoed on repeat for hours as the night became cold and the stars burned bright. I shivered in the field as the loneliness finally crept in and consumed me.

I had nothing left. I had no one. I had no purpose anymore.

"Just let me die."

"Never, my child."

I sniffled. "Then, help me be happy, Father."

I could feel his smirk grow as I let the walls I had held up for years to keep him out come down. I could feel the weight of the world release from my shoulders as my brain buzzed with a plan that I wanted to fulfill as he whispered it to me. I knew what I had to do now. I needed to bed Eric and bear a child to make him mine and release my father from his prison. Aislynn would need to be gone for me to be able to have him to myself. I needed to stop their wedding before the gods granted them what should've been mine. Eric and I were meant to be together and conquer the world.

It was meant to be us.
It will be us.
Eric is mine.

Chapter 19
Eric Greystone

I needed to talk to Aislynn. We needed to postpone our wedding. We could not swear our marriage with a tainted blade. She had no idea the trauma that dagger held on me, and she would surely understand that we would need to forge a new one before our ceremony.

My brain felt sick with too many memories, old, new, and future thoughts haunting me. I could never give my child that dagger to pass on.

I just needed time to process tonight's events.

I just needed time.

Time, the one true thing an immortal had forever of. It was sickening, and I just wanted to redo the night the planets first aligned and save my family and all the Cambridge ladies from their tragic memories and fate.

I never knew what damage Mags being alive kept Ragnar from completing at his full potential. But something about keeping her alive was key to saving our world.

I straightened my shirt and wiped my lips to free myself from the dishonesty that they held. I swallowed hard as I saw Aislynn standing in the doorway under the moonlight. I inhaled heavily before meeting her. She seemed worried as I grabbed her and carried her into our home, holding her tight against me, trying to rid the emotions from me and let her goodness spread back over me.

"I missed you, my love," she whispered in my ear, as she kissed my neck gently.

I groaned as I walked with her to our room. I needed a release and an explanation as to how the hell she had that dagger for this long without telling me.

I already knew that tonight's sleep was not going to happen. Instead, I wanted to rediscover every part of her body. Maybe it was from my secret betrayal, or maybe it was my inner demons that needed to be released. Either way, the morning would be left for explaining how she even had the dagger that destroyed my family.

When she began to stir, I felt relief wash over me. I had spent the night wide awake and replaying the night's events.

I could still feel Izzy's lips on mine and was angry with myself for betraying my love, but also it still felt necessary. Something about Izzy made me feel connected to her, and I wanted to know why.

"Morning, love," I whispered.

Aislynn stirred quietly next to me and smiled before opening her eyes. "Morning."

I pulled her back into my arms and held her for a moment longer before breaking the news that had kept me up all night. I knew she wasn't going to like it, but I also knew that she was going to have to accept it, otherwise we would be doomed from the start with bad luck.

I sucked in a breath and held it. "My love…"

She opened her eyes and looked back at me with concern. "What's happened?" She sat up and faced me.

I shook my head and frowned. "That dagger cannot be used for our ceremony."

She looked back at me, confused. "You looked at it?"

"Well, it fell out of the cloth."

She sat back and shook her head. "Then, we surely cannot use it. I will speak to my mother and get a better one." She looked out toward the window and turned back to me with sadness. "We will have to postpone the ceremony. I swear I do not have cold feet, but that exchange is important for our children to have to pass on. We cannot seal our marriage without a sword fit for our family."

I sat there, shocked that I had not said anything yet, but she only knew half the truth. I sat there and wanted to tell her more, but I did not want her knowing that a weapon was my weakness. But I also knew that the Hildisvini dagger would need to stay safe in our home from this day forward. I needed time to decide when the right moment would be. I would need to seal it away somewhere so that no one, not even Izzy, could ever find it again. I would need to keep Ragnar locked away. I knew my true task would be to kill him one day. Selfishly, I wanted to live my life with Ais before I had to face the unknown consequence of killing him.

I shook my head and debated on when the best time would be.

There was truly no good time. My mind raced.

What if he was getting stronger?

What if he had a plan to get out?

What if I can't reach him when I'm ready to?

What if he gets out and kills my unborn children or my wife?

I can't wait.

Can I wait?

I inhaled heavily and knew that it would be my secret to bear, and I could never let anyone take the dagger away from my sight. A burden that would be sealed for my eternity. It was only to be mine to bear. It could be my apology to Ragnar's mother for never fixing the broken one. I was doing her a favor by doing what Izzy asked of me to keep the dagger far away from her.

Wasn't that enough?

I was sure that Izzy was long gone by now, and a part of me was thankful for the distance, but then my forearm tingled as I thought of her being alone.

I looked down at my Mark and rubbed it gently, trying to erase my past and just focus on my future with my Aislynn instead. I smiled when I looked back at her and knew that no matter what, she wanted to share my surname.

I nodded and let her fall back to sleep while I got up and grabbed the dagger, needing advice from someone level headed. I marched over to Oxana's home, where my brother and Mags were staying.

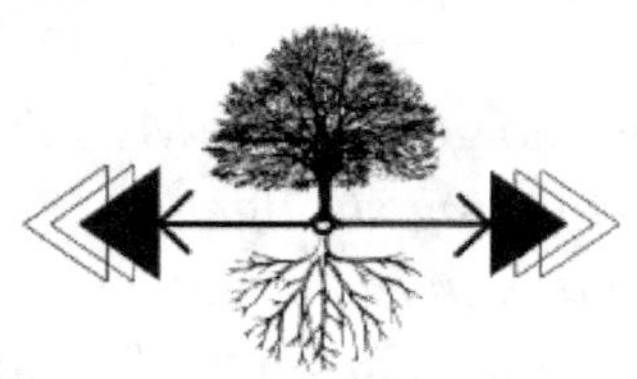

"You're calling it off or postponing it?" Jimmy asked angrily.

"No, just postponing it."

I grasped the dagger and removed the cloth. I watched as both Mags and my brother gasped. Oxana walked into the room and nearly fell backward when she saw the shimmering obsidian blade before her.

"Where did you get that?" she exclaimed with anger, as she came and grabbed it from me. "Is he still trapped?"

I nodded reassuringly and snatched it back from her. "Yes, he should be."

"Should be? Or is?" She yelled.

I shushed her. "Be quiet." I rolled my eyes. "He is still trapped. Aislynn was to use this dagger in our wedding ceremony. It's from her family."

Oxana nodded. "I knew they made it, but why did she have it?" Oxana began to pace back and forth. "I grabbed that dagger that day and instructed her mother to sink it at sea. It was never to resurface again."

I shook my head. "Well, she must not've."

She shook her head. I watched as Mags kept her distance from the dagger that was supposed to take her life. She swallowed hard as she stood and walked to the window.

"Does she know I'm here?" Mags asked.

"No, she has no idea that you are alive."

Jimmy huffed. "You talked to her?" He got up and grasped my shoulders, throwing me back against the wall. "You talked to her and let her live?" His strength was immaculate when he was angry, if only he would use his power more often to master his potential.

I smirked as I grabbed his wrists and pushed him off me, throwing him to the ground with the strength I had trained with and mastered. I stepped on his throat and pinned him in place. "Don't ever test me again."

He groaned underneath me and put his hands up in surrender.

"You need to use your magic more, brother. You are stronger than me if you would just open up your power."

I lifted my foot off him and lent him a hand, pulling him back to his feet.

"I don't want this power. You were right when you said immortality sucks without our loved ones." He looked over to Mags and frowned. "Not you, but without our parents."

She nodded. "I feel the same way." She twisted her Labradorite necklace and squeezed it tight in her palm.

"Okay, so you talked to Izzy and she knows nothing?" Jimmy asked.

I cleared my throat. "Well, she knows we have the dagger."

Mags gasped and dropped her grip, letting the stone shimmer on her chest, blinding me with the sunlight's glare. "We need to leave. Now." She began to head upstairs. I grabbed her wrist, Jimmy eyeing me angrily as I pulled her back to us.

"Let her go," Jimmy growled.

"No, you need to listen to me."

"Alright." Mags looked between my brother and I and nodded. "What're you thinking?"

I inhaled heavily. "I'm going to destroy the dagger."

Mags laughed. "That's your brilliant plan?"

I glared back at her and was regretting that she hadn't gone to pack her shit to leave, scared and running like she had been for a decade.

"You can't just destroy it." She swallowed and pleaded for me to listen. "My mother always thought I was too childish to know what was happening, but instead, I was a fly on the wall. I heard everything. I listened and absorbed her words." She shrugged innocently. "She trapped my father in there so that one day, you and him would be able to kill him." She pointed

174

to Jimmy as her eyes saddened. "Our mothers wanted you both to have immortality as a failsafe in case my father was too strong for you. They wanted you both to have a fighting chance against him. The dagger cannot be destroyed until he is killed or unleashed from it. She made sure that he couldn't escape it, and destroying it would only give him an easier out as the seal would no longer be concealing him."

"But, of course, you don't want your precious lover boy to get killed in the process. So selfishly, you wanted to wait until I could kill him myself. Am I right?"

She looked away from Jimmy and back to me with pleading eyes. "Yes, selfishly, I didn't want to lose anyone else in my life. I would gladly let you die if it meant that your brother could live."

I huffed. "My brother and I were made to be immortal to kill your father together. That was our mission to finish *together*."

Jimmy nodded. "He's right." He turned around and paced. "We've had a decade to ourselves, and we have lived and traveled and loved. But he is right. My brother and I promised Oxana that we would finish the job our parents wanted us to."

Oxana stayed deep in thought.

"Yeah, but with you hiding your magic instead of growing it, you've royally screwed us from defeating him," I said.

"You don't even know how to get to him," Jimmy sneered back at me.

I shook my head. "I have a theory."

"What's that?"

"I think I can transport there." I pointed to my head.

Mags sighed. "I think you're right." She half smiled at me. "You have a strong mind, and you are able to create worlds with yours. Your brother told me how you created the middle for him to go to as a safe space as a child. I'm betting that is exactly how you can get into that dagger. If my father knows that you can get in there to destroy him, he will do everything in his power to push you out of it. You will have one chance before he seals you out of there."

My brother nodded. "When?"

I looked between the three of them as Oxana stayed silent with her secrets.

A flash of Aislynn laying in my field with our unborn children came to mind, and the thought of any danger against them made my rage surface. I could not start a family with her until I knew that she would forever be safe in our world.

"Tonight." I clenched my jaw and exhaled.

Jimmy nodded and shook my hand. "Give me the last few hours to prepare myself."

I nodded.

I knew Oxana had more to say but was staying silent, which provoked my anger more. I watched as Mags and my brother made their way upstairs to discuss the next events.

I walked to Oxana and pulled her arm to a halt. "What are you hiding?"

She sniffled and exhaled slowly. "Your brother is not ready."

I huffed. "Tell me something I don't know."

She half smiled. "You are wise beyond your years. I can't ask you to sacrifice yourself to save the world from Ragnar."

"Do you think I can do it alone?"

She frowned. "That's out of the question."

I glared.

She inhaled heavily, "But I do think you can kill him on your own."

I nodded. "I already planned on going in alone."

She shook her head. "Not alone."

She grabbed my hand and rubbed it gently. I watched as her eyes glistened, and a flame appeared in her pupil as she smiled. "I will join you, until the end."

"I can't ask that of you."

She kissed my cheek. "You didn't ask." She pulled back and smiled. "Plus, I haven't been able to stretch my wings in a decade. It would be nice to fly freely and continue to go unnoticed to our world here."

I looked away from her. She had become a mother to me over the last decade. I could never let her die after all she did to try and protect our lands before. I kissed her cheek and nodded, knowing damn well that I was going to go alone. This was my fight, and I was the only one that could kill him in the dagger world.

"Let me get some rest before we go. It's been a long time since I shifted."

I nodded. "Thank you, Oxana. For everything." I pulled her in for a hug and kissed her cheek.

She smiled and turned to walk back inside.

I tightened my grip around the dagger as I headed back to my home. I walked up the stairs quietly as I tried to let my lady stay sound asleep. I slowly opened the door and laid down next to her. Pulling her into my arms and kissing her neck gently, the smell of jasmine and thyme flooded my nose, her scent would help me get through what I had to do.

I kissed her forehead and grabbed my armor before closing the door quietly behind me.

I sat in the field under the lone tree. A part of me was hoping that Izzy would've been there just to apologize before leaving **again.** But it was too late. I needed to do this on my own. I needed to free everyone from the wrath that Ragnar could bring to us all.

I sharpened the Hildisvini blade as I watched the obsidian shimmer under the sun. I focused on the sharp edge as I closed my eyes and opened my mind.

The earth beneath me began to shake, and I could feel my body transport into another dimension. My body began to tremble as the weight on my shoulders felt heavier, and I no longer felt alone. I opened my eyes and realized that I had been followed.

"What the fuck are you doing here?"

Isadora Cambridge

I saw him sitting there under the tree. I wanted to get further away from him until my head felt more clear, but then I heard him.

"It's time… Follow him."

I shook my head and began to turn the opposite way.

"Damn it, Syphon. It's my turn."

It felt as if my soul left me, and I began to float above my own body, watching from afar as my body ran toward Eric. My hands grasped his shoulders as the smirk on my face grew, and the sickening in my stomach wanted to spew out. The field began to spin as I was ripped back into my body, but we were no longer in our Crystal Rock…

"What the fuck are you doing here?" Eric yelled.

I stepped back and looked at my arms as I was alive in one piece. I could hear my father's voice guide my words. "I'm here to help you kill him."

I swallowed hard as I realized this world had no life like ours did. It seemed like the field still, but the storm clouds above us were frightening, and something inside this place felt evil.

"I don't want your help," he snapped.

I shrugged. "Too bad, it's you and me until the end," my father whispered through me like an echo.

His brows furrowed as his brain started to rapid fire.

"Fine, new plan then." He scratched his head and paced. "Can you lure him to this field?"

I nodded. "Of course I can." I tried to bite my tongue, but the hold my father had over me in here was strong.

He exhaled quickly. "Okay." He swallowed hard. "Iz, I'm trusting you. Please don't make me regret it."

"Oh, he's going to regret everything about you." My father chuckled as the pit in my stomach grew.

I nodded and ran in the direction that my instincts told me not to go.

I froze as I saw a figure walking toward me.

But it was too late. I could see the scar on his face and the smirk that grew wider as he reached me.

"What took you so long?" my father growled in my ear, as he embraced me, squeezing me as if he were trying to syphon the life out of me.

I had nothing to say, and my body couldn't move.

"It's time for me to take what is mine. The Greystones have ruined everything for me, and your wretched mother can stay trapped he—"

He stopped talking as my eyes widened.

"She's here? Mother's here?" I could feel excitement grow as he stared back at me in disgust.

"You help me escape, and you can have her back."

I shook my head. "You don't understand."

He shook me in anger. "I don't understand what?"

"I can't help you get out of here."

"Liar," he screamed, spitting in my face. "Get me out of this prison now, Syphon!"

I swallowed hard. "I can't."

"Tell me the truth. Tell me what you know."

I shook my head, wanting to run and get out of here. I wanted nothing more to do with him. "I don't know."

He scoffed. "You know something."

"I don't."

His anger engaged as he took me by the back of my head and slammed me against a tree. "Tell me."

Tears filled my eyes as I shook my head, trying to keep the secret to myself. Trying to save Eric the only way I knew how. I could not let him get close to him. He would kill him, and it would be another life on my hands that I would regret.

"Tell me."

My brain buzzed as I no longer felt in control of my own thoughts, and my lips began to move. "I can't get you out of here, only the blood of an heir can release you. I have no child, and Mags is dead. You trapped yourself," I spat. "I will never bear a child to help you escape this place."

He let go of my head and breathed heavily as he began to pace.

"A child?" he spat, as he shook his head. "Your mother was more clever than I expected." He punched the air and swore to the skies. "Damn her."

I rubbed the back of my head and felt the advantage grow. "Mother is here?"

He stopped pacing and turned to glare at me. "She will stay trapped until you bring me a grandsire."

I shook my head. "I can't."

He smirked. "You might not be able to do it yourself, but I will make sure it happens." He grabbed my wrist and dragged me hard toward him. "You might not be able to seduce Eric, but I bet Aislynn Meadows can." He gritted his teeth at her name and forced his hands across my head as he spewed incantations I never heard before.

My body began to tingle as I felt the magic flowing through me. I could feel it transform me into someone I was not.

I looked down through his grasp and watched as my Mark disappeared and my hands became unknown to me.

He let go of me and threw me back against the ground.

"There, Aislynn Meadows. Now seduce the man that you love and release me." He smirked, and the scar grew as he smiled. "As soon as that fetus is big enough in your womb, you use the dagger and release me."

I shook my head. "What have you done? What did you do?" I shook my head, and my body shook uncontrollably. "You're a monster. You are everything they say in the stories to scare children. You are nothing but pure evil." I jumped up. "I hate you. I hate you. I hate you!" I screamed, as I tried to grow a flame with shaking palms that were not mine.

He laughed as I failed. Again.

"You are Aislynn Meadows, and it is time to conceive a child with Eric Greystone. Leave this world, and don't come back until you have a child to release me."

I felt my brain tingle as I began to walk back to the field.

Then, I nodded with my mission in mind as he followed me.

I saw the clearing of the field come into view. I froze when I saw Eric drop to his knees, defeated, as my father pulled a blade from behind me and placed it across my chest, against my throat.

"Eric Greystone, how dare you bring your lover into my prison. Not very smart for a warrior, are you?" My father taunted him.

I tried to speak, but my words were being held back by his mind games. I tried to shake my head, but his blade pressed tighter against my neck.

"Don't fail me again, Syphon," he growled into my ear, as tears streamed down my face.

Eric sheathed the dagger and walked slowly toward us with his hands in the air for surrender.

"Please, don't hurt her. Just let her go. She is innocent in all of this," Eric pleaded, as he inched closer.

My father turned me around in his grasp and smirked down at me. "Do as I say, otherwise I will kill your mother."

My eyes widened, and I gasped.

He was the master of manipulation and seemed to hold all the cards again. I had nothing out of this world, and the dream of having my mother back would be something again.

"Turn off your humanity. Focus on saving me and your mother. Nothing else matters. Stop the tears, and make me proud."

I closed my eyes and let the last tear fall as he turned me back around and pushed me toward Eric, letting me fall hard to the ground. I felt Eric grasp my arm and pull me up into his arms as he exhaled shakily.

"Where's Izzy?" he yelled back at Ragnar.

"Dead. You let her down again. Such a great friend you are. Thanks for bringing my family back together again," Ragnar taunted Eric as he smiled wide, making his scar glisten.

Eric's chest shook as he squeezed me tighter against him. "Damn you."

I wanted to tell him, but there was a power hanging over me that kept my mouth shut.

He closed his eyes as we were ripped from the prison world and dropped back home under the tree in the field. He held me close as he sobbed, and I could *feel* his heart breaking as if it were my own.

"I failed her," Eric cried.

Any other part of me would have comforted him, but I saw the weakness he was portraying and knew it was my turn to take advantage of it.

I lifted his chin and brought his attention back to *Aislynn Meadows,* here I was, the love of his life.

"We're safe," I whispered, as he pulled me against him. "Make love to me."

He pulled back away from me and studied my face, clearing his throat.

I wiped the tears from his cheeks and kissed his eyes.

"You saved me," I whispered. "I want you to make love to me right here." I kissed his lips. "Please, you almost lost me too," I pleaded, as I laid down with him under the full moon and smiled as I pulled him on top of me.

"Ais…" he whispered. "I can't right now. I just lost my friend."

I nodded. "We can grieve for her in the morning. Right now, I want to feel you with me."

I watched as his own physical needs took over his emotions as he ripped my dress down the front, buttons breaking as he began to kiss me back.

I smiled as I looked up at the full moon and emotionlessly let him give me exactly what I *wanted*. I could feel the universe work in my favor as I could feel my Mark begin to tingle again. I smirked as his thrusts continued and my father's plan began to strengthen.

We woke with the sun on our backs as we laid naked under the tree that we had grown up with. I smiled as I looked down and realized my black hair was gone and my blonde braids bounced upon my nipples as I sat back up. Eric was sleeping soundly next to me.

"What have I done?" I whispered, as my hand went to my belly. I could feel the magic already growing inside me.

"Won't be long now, Syphon."

"No." I yelled, as I realized what had happened. "What have you done?" I yelled and stood up frantically. "I can't bear a child. I don't want this. Our cursed bloodline was to end with me."

My father already ruined me, and now he was taking Eric down with me.

My body began to shake as I fumbled for my torn clothes and tried to hide my shame.

Eric sat up quickly and refocused on his surroundings.

"Izzy?" He jumped up and lifted his pants. "Izzy?" He stared at me in confusion. "I thought you were dead… Your father said—"

I froze as he saw me trying to fumble with my clothes.

"Ais… Where's Ais?" He looked around the field and turned back at me and glared. "What have you done?" he snarled.

"I'm sorry," I shrieked, as my head pounded. "You have months to tell her… it had to be done." I grabbed my belly and held it protectively.

He looked from me to my hands and dropped to his knees.

"Why?" He asked in defeat.

"I need this."

"Isadora Cambridge, I never want to see you again. That child was made out of trickery and will be just like your father. That was not love—that was evil. You are just like him." He shook his head and pounded the ground.

"You have months to tell Aislynn. You can either raise your child or stay with that pagan whore." I was shocked at my own words that began to spew. "You were mine to marry and have a family with. Not her. Now it is done. You are to be mine. You are mine!" I wanted to cry, but my mind wouldn't let me feel the regret that I reached for.

He shook his head and grabbed the dagger from his sheath as he charged me. He pinned me against the ground and raised the dagger in the air, ready to lunge it into my belly. My mind raced as I tried to fight him off. His strength was impossible to fight off, if only I had my syphoning to steal it from him.

"It's your child. Would you kill your own child? What evil is that?"

He gasped with sweat and rage as he fought his own demons. He lowered the blade and let it drop from his hand, before rolling off me and breathing heavily while staring into the sky.

"Why?" he asked.

"I had to."

He growled next to me. "I will tell her myself…" He breathed heavily, holding back his sadness. "When the time is right."

I sat up and exhaled with relief. "You will be happy." I placed his hand on my belly.

He ripped his hand away from me. "Don't." He stood up and pointed back at me. "I will never love you. Do you understand me? You trapped me. That is *not* love."

I took his hand and pulled myself up with him. "I know you feel the connection too. Look at your Mark, it matches mine. We were meant for this. This is our fate. We were supposed to be together, and now we will be." I felt torn between wanting and needing this. I could feel my own demons battling inside me as to what was right. I leaned in and kissed his cheek. I watched as his face seemed in torment, but even he couldn't deny the connection.

He looked down at the ground and nodded. "I feel something with you… it's just not love."

I shrugged. "Love was never my thing anyway." My inner good snapped like the weak twig at the market last spring. I grabbed my tourmaline necklace and ripped it off, tossing it across the field.

Goodbye, Isadora Camrbridge, weak, caring, worthless twin.

He looked back at me and seemed shocked.

"I miss the old you."

I smirked. "Yeah, well, the old me was easy to break and manipulate." I smiled. "Now, look at me. Beautiful, glowing, and now I own you." I chuckled. "Honestly, I, for once, feel happy. Be happy for me."

He swallowed hard and looked away.

"I said, be happy for me." I pulled the dagger from the ground and held it out toward his neck.

"Do it," he urged.

I pressed the blade harder against his throat and smiled. "I'm not done with you yet."

He looked back at me and half smiled. "I'm glad my end became your happiness. Selfish, just like your father was." He shook his head. "Goodbye, Isadora."

"See you in nine months, lover boy."

He began to walk away and then stopped. "I hope that child has my heart and is nothing like you."

I snorted, as his words meant nothing to me, and tossed the dagger back at him, knowing that we were destined to be together again. He could carry the burden while I carried his heir.

"Now look who the coward is," I yelled, as he bent down to grab it. He turned back in anger as I smirked. "Goodbye, Eric. Just like the sun and moon, you and I *should* never be together again. But now," I winked and grabbed my belly. "Now, we *will* be. Always."

Chapter 21
Eric Greystone

I had held the secret for eight months, and I knew each day was reaching closer to my child being born. Aislynn was still the proud lady of my life that was ready for our wedding. We had made it through another brutal winter, and spring was back in bloom. If only she knew of the deceit I caused her. Then, she would never speak to me again.

I had one last longship trip to take today, and I would be back by tomorrow. I made it my mission to tell her then. If she wanted to leave me, then at least I could know that we had not had an official ceremony yet and she could start her life over in a new town far away from me.

"Just a few drops of blood. I will track your journey to make sure you are coming home safe."

I nodded and gave her my hand. She sliced my finger and collected the drops in the vile carefully. "You're sure you don't want to join me?"

She smiled. "Your crew isn't very fond of an unwed woman on their ship, remember?"

I rolled my eyes. "The keywords are 'my ship,' meaning my rules."

She laughed. "Just come back safe to me."

I nodded and kissed her lips before walking away.

Oxana hadn't spoken to me since I took the dagger world trip on my own. She was furious that I had ruined our one chance at killing Ragnar without him knowing we could access him. Now each time I had tried to enter the world, I was thrown back out with a new scar each time. I could feel that he was getting stronger, and I assumed that Izzy had something to do with it. I gritted my teeth as I walked past Oxana's home.

My brother and Mags had not been back since last spring, and last I heard, they had continued in hiding and would come back when they felt it was safe again.

I shrugged as I felt the loneliness of the world creep into me.

The trip was mere hours on the river as I watched Greystone land come back into view. I was happy to see

Aislynn waiting for me by the shores. I smiled and waved as we docked. I sucked in a heavy breath and knew that I would have to tell her today.

"You look like hell," she whispered, as she kissed me. "Maybe a rest is needed."

I laughed and picked her up, carrying her back to our home. I hadn't meant to, but my mind was tired as I closed my eyes and let hours pass.

It was the blood curdling scream that woke me from outside. The sun was beginning to set while I glanced out of the window and saw Izzy, holding her enlarged belly, bleeding and walking down the dirt road. Cursing Aislynn's name as she burned our door and broke through it.

"She tried to kill me," Izzy screamed.

I stepped between the two of them and forced them apart.

"No, I did kill her," Aislynn spat back. "She had no pulse."

"Here I am, live and well, you pagan bitch," Izzy spat, as she charged her palms with fire and tried to burn Aislynn.

I lifted my arm as my Mark began to glow through the ink and caught the flame, cooling my forearm as if it were nothing of danger.

Both women froze as they watched my Mark glow and then Izzy's did the same.

"Is it yours?" Aislynn screamed and pointed to Izzy's belly.

I tried to calm her, but she became frantic. "I tracked her with your blood. It led me straight to her, a town away. It's yours… isn't it?" Aislynn began to sob. "You called off our wedding because of that thing… Didn't you?"

I grabbed her arms and tried to calm her. "No, love, no… it's–"

"It's his child." Izzy taunted Aislynn. "He made sure to make the sweetest love to me on what should've been your wedding night."

I turned and pushed Izzy against the wall and spit in anger. "You tricked me!"

Izzy laughed demonically as she smiled back at Aislynn. "He's mine now."

Aislynn became enraged as she grabbed the Hildisvini dagger and screamed incantations to it before she ran past me and plunged the blade into my unborn heir.

"No," I yelled, as I tried to stop her.

Izzy screamed as she heard the words of Aislynn's spell. "You will be infertile from this day on. You will never bear another child. Your father will never be released from his prison now."

I stepped back and felt my two worlds colliding, as my Mark tried to pull toward Izzy but my heart tugged back to Aislynn. My world felt ready to implode as I watched Aislynn take the dagger that had ruined so much already—my parents, my unborn child.

"How could you hurt me like this?" Ais cried, as she grabbed it and plunged it into her own chest before falling to the ground, and her breathing slowed.

I dropped to my knees and held her against my chest. "Ais… No… What have you done? What have you done?" I rocked back and forth. "Somebody, anybody, help… help me."

I pulled her tighter against my chest as her blood seeped through to my shirt, and prayed that my child could survive and that Aislynn would live. I prayed to the gods and swore to live on the right path if they would only hear me now. I needed them to live.

"Please…" I willed the innocents to breathe again.

When I felt Asilynn's last breath leave her tiny body, I cursed the whole universe so that it would know that I would come for it. I would destroy Ragnar and the entire magic world that ruined my life. I cursed the dagger.

Izzy grabbed my hand and pleaded for me to help her.

As much as I wanted to burn her alive next to me, I felt connected to her still and wanted to keep her safe. I looked down at my Mark as I held her hers and cursed it and any future witches that held the weight of an anchor to be tied to on a sinking ship. Now I knew that an anchor would only drown you faster.

A part of me that would never come back.

I ripped my hand from hers as I let a part of me die that day.

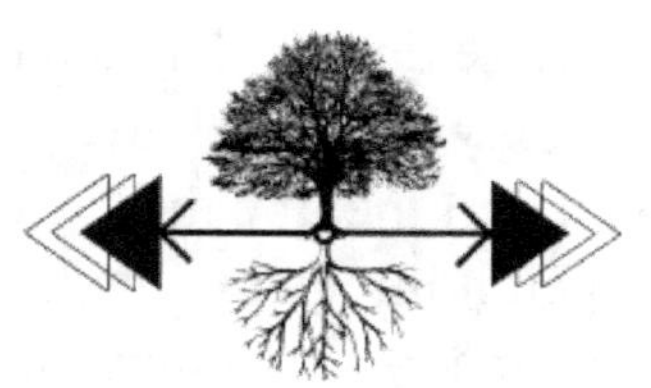

Rumors began to spread as people in my own town made up their own stories of Izzy and me. They began to say that we had gone mad and sacrificed Aislynn and an unborn child for power. There was the cursed dagger that went missing when I went back home to find it. Both Aislynn's body and the dagger disappeared. Her mother was rumored to take them away for proper burial. Even Oxana didn't defend me and let me burn with the lies being spread.

I couldn't stay any longer. I needed to get away from my home. So, I ran.

I ran until I no longer had breath left in me to take me further. Then, I let my legs carry me day by day.

It had been weeks since that tragic day, but it was a day I lived over and over again in my head.

I sat silently next to the river and listened as it flowed peacefully. I longed for a home again, anywhere to lay my head and know that it was mine. I wanted my life back. I wanted my Ais back. I wanted the unborn child that I never was able to meet.

I watched as the river rushed and debated on ending it here. But the last time I attempted to provoke a fight with another traveler, I thought I had finally broken my curse, only to wake the next morning healed. I cursed the skies and hated my new life of immortality, one that I would live alone. That's when I heard her voice.

"Still running away?" Izzy came walking up behind me.

"Leave me alone."

She ignored my wishes and sat beside me. "You and I are connected. Don't you feel the pull toward me as I do with you?" She laughed. "I mean, even if I wanted to, I can't seem to leave you alone." She huffed. "I've been following you for weeks… the least you could do is take a shower."

I turned and pinned her against the sand, wanting to choke the life out of her.

"Do it." She smiled. "I'll keep coming back, thanks to this stupid Mark."

I released my grip and stood, putting distance between us.

"You and I are forever. You just need to accept it."

"No." I shook my head in rage. "You and I are nothing."

"Not even friends?" She pouted and then began to laugh.

"Friends don't do what you did."

She stood and gasped. "What *I* did?" She pointed to herself as if I had stabbed her myself. "I gave you the heir you needed, and you turned your back on me. You were supposed to protect me and our child."

I shook my head. "Stop."

"No, you stop." She forced herself in front of me and screamed, "*You* were supposed to be mine, and *you* decided to fall in love with a pagan."

"You were dead!"

She laughed hysterically. "I was far from dead. Instead, I lived a decade trying to stay sane while you were off rebuilding the lands that were supposed to be ours. You fell in love with another. You deserve every bit of pain that you are feeling right now. You were supposed to save Mags from me. So, call it a loss for a loss."

I stepped back and growled. But then I realized she still had no idea that Mags was alive. I breathed in heavily and tried to understand what game she was playing.

"What do you want, Izzy?"

"Want?" She laughed. "I need another child."

I laughed and spat next to her. "Not from me."

"Not naturally, thanks to your dead pagan."

"Watch it." I grabbed her throat and released it.

She smiled. "Oh, a soft spot."

I clenched my jaw and shook my head.

"How do you know that Aislynn wasn't transported to that dagger like my father was?" She raised her eyebrow and smirked.

I huffed. "Lies."

Izzy shrugged. "How sure are you?"

I swallowed hard and stood quietly.

"What if I told you I have a way of getting back into the dagger?"

I glared at her and waited.

"I want that dagger back, and you're going to help me get it."

"Good luck, it's long gone."

She smirked. "Gone or missing?"

"Missing."

"Pagan witches and their games." She shrugged. "Well, it looks like we have to search for it then."

"You're on your own, Iz."

She smiled and pointed to her Mark. "Not really, you and I are fated to be together. Seems like death isn't so permanent for me after all… or you, for that matter." She pointed to my new self-induced scar. "So… you can love me or you can hate me, but either way, you are mine until I say so."

I wanted to kill her. I wanted to rip her blackened heart out and destroy her from whatever link she had with me. But then again, what if my Ais was somehow trapped in that prison world with Ragnar using her however he seemed fit. I also knew that if I stayed with her, then I could make sure she never found my brother or Mags to harm them.

At this point, I had nothing left to lose. I spit in my hand and held it out to her.

"Friends?" she questioned.

I debated on the game she had played and figured it was my turn to join along and keep her guessing. I smirked and held back the rage in my voice.

"Maybe more."

She smiled and spit in her hand before shaking mine and sealing our fate.

Isadora Cambridge

For centuries, Eric and I had the dagger, and we were so close to releasing my parents from the prison world. Time and time again, we failed with every theory and chance we had. A part of me believed him to be self-sabotaging my plan to free them, but then he would give me his word that we were on the same team. He would give himself to me and be a good, obedient lover, then other times, he would torment me with his love of other women—all who seemed to look like Aislynn Meadows with dark hair and goddess skin. It made me sick that he would never let her go. But then again… I'd won. He was mine. Whenever he would get too close to one of the women, I would use the dagger to free him from their fake love.

I loved watching him in torment and pretending to not have a care in the world.

It was finally when his brother had gone missing that he finally seemed to have a switch in his behavior. Rumors spread that Jimmy was sacrificed by another pagan witch, and I smiled knowing that Eric's hate for pagans would grow with the loss of his brother. His immortality didn't survive without an Anchor like we had. Oxana had failed Jimmy, just as she had failed everyone else.

I smiled until one day… Alexandra Chamberlain came around.

Why Eric had such a hold on her blew my mind. She was an Anchor witch but had nothing more than the power of persuasion, and of course, Eric let her into his head. She was using him, and it was only a matter of time until I would send her to the prison world for my father. Eric was never going to be hers to control.

I thought he would finally leave her alone when she became pregnant by her mundane husband. But instead, he became more intrigued by her. In his years of fathering the orphan, Declan, his heart was becoming softer, and it made me sick that he thought he knew what love was.

I had planned to kill Clara, Alexandra's precious Anchor, right before I could get my revenge on Alexandra. I was on my way to the warehouse where Eric had been holding Clara when he called and said they got away with *my* dagger.

It was that day that my father's voice reappeared to me after years of silence from feeding him the souls with the dagger. He was quiet and consuming his strength.

But now… He was angry with me. He was tormenting my brain every hour it was missing as I frantically tried to find it.

My father would not rest until I had the dagger back in my possession.

So, if Alexandra wouldn't bring it back to town, then I'd just have to lure her back to it.

I told Eric of my plan, and he was not pleased with involving children. He made me promise to not harm her child. I rolled my eyes and didn't understand what hold the stupid girl had on him, considering she wasn't anything special. She didn't even have any magic. A mundane who was worthless.

But, to make him happy, I agreed to let her live… for a while anyway.

I heard the soft knock of a cowardly child on my door and smiled.

I straightened my glasses, fluffed my blonde curls out and grabbed my heels from under my desk of the makeshift closet of a room that I claimed to be a therapist's office. I cleared my throat as I walked toward the door.

I opened it with a confident smile as I looked at the broken little child that just lost the love of her life. I knew that she would surely be easy to crack. No time at all, and her pathetic mother would be back in town with my prized possession.

I tried to give her an apologetic look, even though I knew exactly what had happened to her and who had killed her little Jaxon lover boy. Tragic, really… Jaxon, with his beautiful blue eyes. But it had to be done. Love was a weakness, and she would surely thank me one day when she became stronger.

I held my laugh in as I remembered my little minion semi-truck driver did exactly as he was told to do. Compulsion spells were becoming too easy on the weak. Of course, I had to keep Eric out of the loop for a little while on that one. At least, while I manipulated this little child into bringing her dear old, ragged, awful mother back to town with my dagger.

"Ms. Chamberlain, please do come in," I greeted her with sad eyes and held back my smirk.

Closing the door behind me, I grinned, knowing that soon enough, I would finally be able to release my mother from the hell she'd been stuck in and then I could kill Ms. Freya and all of her family for delaying my very own family reunion.

What's next?

One final chapter…
Find out what happens to your
favorite characters in the finale
Bonds & Bones

For more information on the series check
out the author website for future updates:

https://stephanievorwald.wixsite.com/website

ABOUT THE AUTHOR

Stephanie Vorwald is the author of the Witches & Immortals Series. She found her passion for writing long before she achieved writing 'The End' for her debut novel. She loves writing fantasy books where she can create her own world of magic in everyday, ordinary life. When she is not writing, she is a Registered Dental Hygienist. She loves being a mother to her kids and having family time.